"SO WHY ARE you doing this?" Danny asked.

For the next twenty minutes the man explained exactly why they had taken Steph. And what they wanted him to do to get her back.

Now that Danny was in Phoenix, he knew he couldn't do what they were asking.

He just couldn't.

But it seemed he had no choice.

He had to call the police. He had to have help.

He picked up the phone, then put it back down, the man's voice echoing in his ears. "Trust me," the man had said, "you call the police and we can kill your wife before you hang up the phone."

Those words echoed through his mind. How would they know if he called the police?

He couldn't take the chance.

The image of Steph's face filled his mind and he moved over to the couch and sat down.

It was going to be a very long night.

And an even longer golf tournament.

Also by
Dean Wesley Smith

The Cold Poker Gang Mysteries:

Kill Game
Cold Call
Calling Dead
Bad Beat
Dead Hand

Doc Hill:

Dead Money
"The Road Back"

AN
EASY
SHOT

DEAN WESLEY SMITH

*wmg*PUBLISHING

An Easy Shot

Published 2016 by WMG Publishing
www.wmgpublishing.com
First published as a serialized novel beginning March 2015
in *Smith's Monthly,* WMG Publishing
Cover and layout copyright © 2016 by WMG Publishing
Cover design by Allyson Longueira/WMG Publishing
Cover art copyright © Fotoslaz/Dreamstime
ISBN-13: 978-1-56146-760-0
ISBN-10: 1-56146-760-X

For KKR, always the love of my life

AN
EASY
SHOT

PROLOGUE

_____

Monday, April 3rd
11:12 p.m.

CHARLES ROBINS IGNORED the crisp desert air and the star-filled Arizona night as he stepped onto the stone patio of his Scottsdale mansion. His entire focus was on the dark-suited man who leaned against a rock wall, smoking.

Beyond the wall, the lights of Phoenix stretched out across the valley floor. Often, on spring nights like this, Charles would have his after-dinner brandy served on this patio. He loved the view, the lights, the feeling of being above all the masses below.

But not tonight.

At the moment there was much more important business to attend to. There would always be other warm nights and brandy on the patio.

The man dropped the red-tipped cigarette and ground it under his foot as Charles closed the patio door and turned.

The man would fit into most crowds. His dark suit wasn't expensive, but it wasn't cheap either. His face was clean shaven and had nothing really distinctive about it. His hair was short and he was going slightly bald. Charles doubted he would even recognize the man if they passed on the street. Yet the man was one of Charles's most trusted and valued employees.

The man waited, making Charles come to him. No one else could do that. Charles controlled businesses worth a billion dollars, had twenty servants and six body guards in this house alone, and was considered one of the most eligible bachelors in the country. Yet this man just didn't seem to care.

Charles asked him to do special tasks, paid him well, and that was all the man did. He scared Charles by his very coldness. No one else in this world did that to Charles.

In the three years the man had worked for Charles, this was only their fourth meeting. All four meetings had been on this patio, and always alone. Charles didn't even know the man's real name and had no desire to learn it. Charles just called him Bill when he had to call him anything at all, and the man didn't seem to care. Yet Charles knew to the penny how many hundreds of thousands of dollars this man, under a false company name, had been paid for "consulting."

And every penny had been worth it.

The man spoke little, and Charles liked that about him. Tonight there were no greetings. The man, his dark eyes hidden in the faint light, simply stood and waited, his hands behind his back, as if he were in control.

That attitude made Charles feel even less sure about what he was about to do, but at this point he could see no other choice.

"Senator Knight from California will be playing in a pro-am golf tournament here in Scottsdale this weekend," Charles said, keeping his voice low so that it wouldn't carry in the desert air. "Then he will be flying to Washington for a vote Monday morning."

The man said nothing.

Charles went on. "I want you to make sure he doesn't make that trip."

"Never make the trip?" the man asked, his voice very low and deep. "Or delayed?"

"I don't honestly care," Charles said. And he didn't. Senator Kelly had been after him for years. Having the man permanently out of the picture would not be a bad thing. But it was critical Kelly didn't make that vote.

"Understood," the man said, nodding once. "Is that all?"

"Make it look like an accident if you can," Charles said. "But if you can't just make sure it's done. He cannot be allowed to be in Washington on Monday. Understood?"

Again the man nodded once. "This is a United States Senator you are talking about. It will cost you more."

"Of course," Charles said. "Just get it done."

Without even a nod the man turned and started down the rock path beside the garage wall. The night seemed to swallow him. One moment there, the next gone. How the man got past Grant and his men, and in and out of the estate's security system was another question Charles just didn't want to know the answer to.

Charles stared after the man for a moment, feeling uncertain, and very worried, just as he had felt every other time he had talked to him. Yet the man always got the task done.

Charles turned to look out over the lights of the valley below. This mansion, all his property, everything he owned and controlled, was being threatened and he couldn't let that happen. Senator Kelly was the push behind legislation that would cripple two of Charles's main companies, and lead to investigations that Charles knew he couldn't withstand. If Senator Kelly's legislation passed, Charles would be broke and fighting to stay out of jail in less than a year.

Most of his waking hours—and many of his nightmares—over the last few months had been to fight this bill. He had wrapped up enough votes in Kelly's committee to tie and kill the bill if Kelly didn't vote. But Chairman Kelly's vote would put the bill on the floor of the Senate and from there it couldn't be stopped.

The key to it all was making sure Senator Kelly didn't make that vote.

Charles glanced down the dark path where the man he called Bill had disappeared. He could see nothing.

With a deep breath of the fresh, crisp night air, Charles turned and headed back inside. He had a lot of work to do and work was always the best thing to take his mind off of what he had just ordered done.

If that was even possible.

***

Friday, April 7th
8:02 a.m.

The three gunmen walked into the small apartment of Steph and Danny Baines without knocking. Two wore masks, the third, who was in charge, didn't seem to care who saw him. But he knew that the residents of the nearby apartments had all left for work. Only twenty-four-year-old Steph Barnes was at home.

The small apartment hugged against the back of a large red rock just above the small valley that held Sedona, Arizona. It had one bedroom, a small living room and kitchen, and a fantastic view of the red-rock country around Sedona from a balcony.

Danny worked as the assistant golf pro for the local country club and Steph taught sixth grade. They were both from Phoenix, had met in college, and were hoping that Danny would get a job this next fall on one of the bigger Scottsdale clubs so they could move back. They both loved Sedona, but it was just too cold in the winter for both of them.

Danny stood just under six feet tall, had sun-bleached brown hair and a smooth-as-silk golf swing. Steph was almost as tall, with light auburn hair and a smile that could melt a sixth-grader. Everyone said they looked more like brother and sister than husband and wife.

Steph had taken the morning off from school to help Danny get ready for the charity tournament in Phoenix. They both had figured that it would be a wonderful opportunity to meet some people who might help them get back into the Phoenix area. And when he learned he was playing with Senator Knight, Danny got even more excited. Steph was going to come down by bus on Saturday and join the group on Sunday. Not only was it going to be a good chance for Danny to make contacts, it was going to be fun as well.

Steph had just dropped a fifth golf shirt into Danny's suitcase when the front door opened. For a moment she thought it was Danny coming back from the course early. Then she heard a strange voice from the doorway.

"Don't scream or nothin'" the voice said. "Just finish packin' for your husband and everything will be just fine."

She spun around to face three men. All were holding machine-gun-like weapons on her.

Somehow she managed to not scream.

Somehow.

CHAPTER ONE

Friday, April 7th
9:20 p.m.

THE WARM DESERT breeze wrapped around Craig Frakes as he stopped to look back up the hill at the lights of the Canyon Hotel nestled into the rocks. After the long winter in Seattle, he couldn't believe he was here in Scottsdale, Arizona, getting ready to play an entire weekend of golf. This had to be a dream. He was sure he would wake up any moment to the sound of rain pounding against the bedroom window.

His wife, Bonnie, stopped beside him and took his hand, also staring up at the resort they were staying in for the next three nights. "Beautiful, isn't it?"

Beautiful didn't really begin to describe it. The Canyon Hotel had been built using the massive brown rocks and the desert hillside as a frame. The architect had nestled the rooms into the canyon walls,

6

mixing large timbers and massive boulders throughout. The main area was a combination of stone, wood, and soft carpets that felt more like a warm cave and a living room than a hotel lobby.

And the fantastic architecture didn't stop at the lobby. Their room—as the hotel called it—was more like a suite, with a light brown leather couch and chair, a massive bed, and a bathroom larger than some apartments he had rented in college. A switch inside the bathroom door sent a waterfall cascading over rocks and down into a large tub. Craig couldn't imagine how every room in the hotel could be as plush as theirs, but he had a hunch every room was.

From where they stood on the path near the first tee of the Canyon Resort Golf Club, the hotel lights filled the night with a soft glow that felt welcoming and warm, barely pushing back the light from the stars and the small crescent moon.

"You know what's really great about being here?" he asked, looking over at his beautiful wife. Her hair seemed to shimmer in the glow from the hotel and she looked almost waif-like in the white shorts and light blouse.

"What?" she asked, smiling at him.

"It's warm," he said, "it's not raining, and my lips are already chapping from the dryness. What more can a guy ask for?"

She laughed, the sound carrying out over the open fairway and lush grass. "Oh, I can think of a few more things."

She squeezed his hand and pulled him away from staring at the hotel and down the dark, paved golf path that led along the right side of the first hole of the course. "Come on, let's go for a walk."

Now that she mentioned it, Craig could think of a few other things he *could* ask for. And knowing Bonnie, he just might be lucky enough tonight to get one of those wishes.

"Going to be tough to see what the golf course is like in the dark," he said.

"I wasn't thinking of looking at the golf course," she said.

"Oh, I like the sound of that," he said, as they topped over a small rise and headed down a shallow hill that slowly blocked the lights of the hotel.

After the last six months of hard work, they had been looking forward to this vacation. They both worked for the Seattle police department. He was a homicide detective, while she had moved off the streets and now worked special services dealing in domestic violence and runaway children.

Everyone said they made the perfect couple. He was six-one and had just turned thirty-one. She was five-two and thirty. Both of them had dark brown hair, but Bonnie's eyes were a deep brown while his were green.

They had met in college and lived together for years before finally getting married. At some point they both wanted children, but so far their jobs kept them too busy.

He stayed in shape by running and lifting weights, while Bonnie liked swimming more. But they were both avid golfers. Bonnie's handicap was three shots lower than Craig's, and she beat him three out of their four outings, something Craig very seldom let her forget. They loved the game and the good-natured rivalry, and when the opportunity to represent the Seattle Police Department in this charity golf tournament came along, they jumped at the chance to get out of the Seattle spring weather and actually play a round of golf without wearing rain gear.

On top of that, this weekend was going to be the first real vacation they had had in over a year. Craig couldn't believe it had been that long. Being a detective never seemed to allow for much free time. And Bonnie's job wasn't any better. At one point earlier this spring she had had over one hundred active cases of children needing homes, abused spouses, and missing children. He marveled at her strength under that heavy a load.

Now here they were, walking on what seemed to be a perfect-temperature evening in Arizona, the cares of police work a long plane ride behind them.

"You're sure being quiet," Bonnie said as they strolled along the dark path, hand in hand.

They were walking slower than he remembered walking in a long time. It felt great. He could feel the tension draining from his back and shoulders.

"Just relaxing and watching the lights of the valley. And enjoying the company."

"How about enjoying the company a little more closely?" she asked, her voice low and sultry and very suggestive. She pulled him and they bumped hips.

Craig could barely see her smile in the dim light. She was teasing him and he was enjoying it.

"This far from the hotel room?" he asked, teasing back. "I'm afraid I just don't know what you have in mind?"

She laughed. "Six years of marriage and you've forgotten what we used to do on the muni course?"

He would never forget those nights, but instead he said, "Hmmm, how about a reminder?"

As the path crested a small rise near a massive boulder, she pulled him off the pavement and around the rock that towered over the edge of the fairway.

The grass on the other side was lush and soft as she pulled him down beside her. He expected it to be damp and cold, like the grass in the Pacific Northwest always was at night, but instead the fairway was dry and slightly warm from the heat of the day. He was starting to like the desert more and more.

The lights from the valley below gave them just enough light to see what they were doing, yet not enough for Craig to worry about being seen from any distance. And the boulder blocked the view to the path.

"This feels wonderful," Bonnie said, rubbing her hands over the ground as she kicked off her shoes.

"I couldn't agree more," he said, wrapping his arms around her and pulling her close for a long, passionate kiss.

His heart was racing and he was short of breath. For some reason he felt too old to be kissing out under the stars. That seemed like a young person's thing. When had he gotten so old?

He pushed the thought away and let the excitement of the moment take him. After a moment, he started to unbutton her blouse, slowly, carefully, not breaking the kiss.

He could feel her skin under his fingers, getting him even more excited than he already was. But he forced himself to try to take his time. In this kind of situation, that was going to be difficult, at best. It had been a long time since they had done something like this.

Too long.

Finally, after what seemed like an eternity of bumbling, he got the last button undone. It felt like a victory, the same as it had with his first girlfriend back in high school.

Bonnie pulled back. "I see you are remembering just fine."

He ran his hand over her breast, enjoying the soft feel of her skin and the silky feel of the bra. She shivered slightly and leaned into his touch.

"I think it's coming back to me," he said, "but I'm still not sure."

She laughed. "Let's be sure."

She pulled off her blouse and tossed it toward the base of the rock, then as he watched, she lay back, lifted her hips, and slipped off her white shorts, tossing them on top of the blouse.

Just the movement of her body in the faint light made him excited.

And the fear of getting caught. That was exciting him even more.

He glanced around, trying to listen *over* the sounds of his beating heart to see if anyone was coming. As far as he could tell, they were alone.

At least for the moment.

"No grass stains this time," she said.

He laughed. Back on one of their early college dates, they had ended up on the golf course, kissing and touching and having a great time late one night. Bonnie had been wearing white shorts like the ones she had just taken off, and they had gotten ruined from grass stains. And since she had been living at home at the time, it had been very embarrassing to explain to her mother.

"You got to admit, getting those grass stains was fun."

"And this isn't?" she asked, smiling.

"I didn't say that."

They kissed, long and hard, a kiss like they hadn't done in some time. Work had just been so much for both of them that sex had often taken a back seat. His hope, and it seemed to be Bonnie's as well, was that this weekend that would change. Sex would become something they focused on and enjoyed. And this was getting the weekend off to a great start as far as he was concerned.

In the faint light, she was fantastically beautiful. The white of her bra and thin panties was like a light beckoning him to come closer. And he obeyed.

Hell, he *wanted* to obey.

He let his hands brush up her legs, over her flat stomach, to her breasts.

She pulled back. "Wait just a minute. You have too many clothes on now."

With that she sat up and pulled on the bottom of his shirt, helping him take it over his head. It ended up in the pile with her clothes. Then she worked at his belt and unzipped his slacks as he took off his shoes.

He lay back, his butt off the ground, as in one smooth motion she pulled his pants off, leaving him laying in the middle of a fairway on the warm grass in only his white underwear.

It was the most excited he could remember feeling since college.

And the most afraid of getting caught.

He had forgotten what that feeling of doing something illegal was like.

The grass was warm and soft against his skin as he ran his hands over it. What the hell. If they got caught, they got caught. It was their vacation, after all. And they were a long way from home.

"Now you have too many clothes," he said.

"Oh, I like this game," she said, giving him a kiss and then pulling away.

As he watched, she unhooked her bra, tossing it aside with the rest of their clothes. The soft light made her skin seem ultra smooth and silky, as if there wasn't a mole or wrinkle anywhere.

"Like what you see?" she asked, looking down at him.

"Much more than like," he said. "How about love? Admire? Adore?"

"You say all the right things," she said, her laugh carrying into the darkness of the desert and golf course. She lay on top of him. The feel of her breasts against his chest was wonderful.

"Nice," she said, pressing her leg into the hardness of his crotch.

He pulled her tight and they kissed again, moving their bodies slowly against each other. He wanted to touch, to stroke every inch of her. He loved the way she felt against him, her soft skin moving slowly against his.

He kept at it until she finally pulled his head up and kissed him long and hard.

He returned the kiss, suddenly not caring if anyone else was nearby or not. She rolled him over on his back and kneeling beside his legs pulled off his underwear with a frantic jerk, flicking them into the air over her head.

"Oh, I like this," she said, running her hands over him.

"You're not the only one," he said. The sensation was wonderful and much more intense than it had been in a long time.

The warm night, the fear of someone nearby, the grass against his back all seemed to vanish as his body pushed upward. Before she was all the way into position he couldn't help himself and started to move up and down under her.

After a wonderful eternity, they lay panting, sweating, both trying to catch what air they could manage.

That had been intense, and wonderful.

He kissed her neck and she shivered. But she didn't move.

He kissed it again and got the same reaction. Only this time she hugged him, being careful to keep him in the same position.

"Wow," he managed to whisper into her ear.

She squeezed him with her entire body. "Yeah. No argument there."

She carefully stretched out her legs and lay down on him, keeping them together as they rolled over so they were facing each other in a full hug. On one side he could feel her soft skin the length of his body, and on his back grass was sticking to his sweaty body.

With the stars above and warm night air around them, it was a moment he didn't want to let go of.

Clearly Bonnie didn't either.

There was no sound of anyone walking toward them.

The night was quiet, so they just lay there, holding each other, not saying anything.

He couldn't remember feeling this good in a long time. It was an absolutely perfect start to the vacation.

He closed his eyes and let his body completely relax.

CHAPTER TWO

Friday, April 7th
9:46 p.m.

DANNY BAINES TOSSED his bag on the hotel bed and looked around. In all his life he had never felt so scared, so alone, so completely out of his mind.

This all had to be a nightmare and he would wake up very shortly.

He walked into the large bathroom and stared in the mirror.

His eyes were red and he looked like he hadn't slept.

Actually he'd had a good night's sleep last night with Steph and this morning had headed to the course to get his clubs and help get ready for the weekend rush of players before he had to leave for Phoenix.

When he got home, he found his bag packed and sitting by the front door. A man he didn't recognize was sitting on the couch, pointing a gun at him.

Steph was nowhere to be found.

He almost went crazy when the guy said they had taken Steph. He stormed at the guy.

"If I shoot you," the guy had said, pointing the gun at Danny, "I have to kill your wife as well."

That stopped Danny.

And then Danny's blood seemed to freeze as the man laughed. "And she's a looker, too. It would be fun doin' her."

"So why are you doing this?" Danny had asked.

For the next twenty minutes the man had explained exactly why they had taken Steph. And what they wanted him to do to get her back.

Then the man had helped him carry his bag to his car, helped him check the apartment to make sure everything was turned off, and then stood there and watched Danny drive away.

Now Danny was in Phoenix, checked into his room, and going crazy. He couldn't do what they were asking.

He just couldn't.

But it seemed he had no choice.

He headed through the bedroom and out into the main area of the small suite.

The phone was sitting on the desk under a mirror. He moved over to it. He had to call the police. He had to have help.

He picked up the phone, then put it back down, the man's voice echoing in his ears. "Trust me," the man had said, "you call the police and we can kill your wife before you hang up the phone."

Those words echoed through his mind. How would they know if he called the police?

He couldn't take the chance.

The image of Steph's face filled his mind and he moved over to the couch and sat down.

It was going to be a very long night.

And an even longer golf tournament.

CHAPTER THREE

Friday, April 7th
9:53 p.m.

BONNIE'S BREATH WAS even against his neck, the grass soft under him, and he wasn't sure if he hadn't even dozed a little. Amazing, falling asleep nude in the middle of a fairway. This just wasn't like him at all.

Suddenly he realized what had woken him up.

Someone was coming!

The sound of a deep, male voice in the distance drifted over them.

He pulled back enough to see his wife's face in the dim light. Her eyes were closed and she seemed to be asleep as well. He could feel their skin sticking together.

He leaned in close to her ear. "I think someone's coming," he whispered, trying not to startle her.

"Oh, damn," she whispered back.

Her eyes snapped open and she rolled away from him.

The stickiness on his stomach had dried his skin against hers and it pulled like removing a bandage.

"How long were we asleep?" she whispered as she grabbed her shoes and the pile of clothes and moved over toward the side of the giant boulder that towered over them and the fairway. If they stayed against the backside of it, they wouldn't be seen from the cart path.

He grabbed his shoes and followed her as again the male voice could clearly be heard. At least two people were coming from the direction of the clubhouse, walking along the same path they had walked.

Bonnie, her back against the tall rock, slipped on her underwear, then shorts. He started to do the same, then realized his underwear was still out in the middle of the fairway where Bonnie had tossed them aside.

He eased away from the rock slightly and glanced toward the clubhouse. The silhouettes of two men could be seen coming up the small rise about a hundred yards away. One was smoking a cigarette and the red tip glowed in the dark.

"Shit!" he said, softly.

Craig pointed at his underwear and Bonnie snickered. If he went back out onto the fairway to get his underwear, he would be seen, so he slipped his pants on without them.

"Watch that zipper," Bonnie whispered as she put on her bra. "I don't want that part hurt."

"Trust me," he whispered back, "neither do I."

She laughed softly and they both sat down with their backs against the rock, waiting for the intruders to pass as they put on their shoes. He felt like a kid again, almost getting caught at something he shouldn't have been doing. His heart was beating hard and he was enjoying the feeling as the two men moved toward them.

This was fun.

And for some reason damn scary at the same time.

The sound of their footsteps seemed very loud, echoing over the grass and desert like irregular drum beats. Neither man had said a word for at least fifty paces. Then one with a high voice and a slight New York accent said, "I still can't believe we're doin' a Senator."

"Believe it," the other man said.

The second man had a deep, distinctive voice that sounded like a musician's.

"I don't much like the idea of the entire fucking government comin' after me."

The two men were even with the rock and passing.

Craig glanced at Bonnie. Her eyes were huge and she was holding her breath just as he was. Suddenly this had turned from fun to something very serious.

"If nothing goes wrong, no one will be coming after you," the deep-voiced one said. "We just make sure it looks like an accident."

"Yeah, sure," the first man said as the two started down the hill away from Bonnie and Craig. "I better be gettin' paid real good for this."

"Trust me," the deep-voiced man said, "you are. We all are."

"We better," the man said. "A senator. This is nuts."

Craig stared at Bonnie as the two men moved on, clearly headed somewhere out on the golf course. He couldn't believe what he had just heard. And he didn't want to think about what those words seemed to mean.

Bonnie finished putting on her shoes and he followed suit, not saying anything. He stood and made sure the men were long out of sight, then went out and grabbed his underwear off the fairway, stuffing them into his pocket as he turned.

He joined Bonnie on the cart path, headed back toward the clubhouse. After about ten steps he whispered, "Did that sound to you like it sounded to me?"

She put her finger up to his mouth and shook her head. "In the room," she whispered, just loud enough for him to hear.

Then she took his hand and they headed toward the beautiful hotel at a much faster pace than the stroll that got them there.

CHAPTER FOUR

Friday, April 7th
10:07 p.m.

THE WALK BACK to the hotel and up to their room seemed to take forever for Bonnie. Her heart was racing and her mind twisting at what they had overheard out on the course. She desperately wanted to talk to Craig about it, but knew that they didn't dare until they were safely in private. Just as they had discovered, voices carried on that golf course, especially at night.

After Craig closed the door behind them in their room, Bonnie dropped down onto the bed, enjoying the softness of the mattress and the silky feel of the bedspread. "Tell me what you heard."

Craig paced between her and the dark television, a frown on his face. "Two men talking about causing a Senator to have an accident."

Bonnie nodded, her stomach now even more in a knot than it was on the walk back. "That's what I heard as well. Could we have misunderstood?"

"I've been wondering the exact same thing," Craig said, still pacing. "And the answer is yes, of course we could. They could have been talking about a game they were playing. Or the word accident could mean something completely different to them."

"Like what?" Bonnie asked, wanting to believe him, but not really following his logic.

Craig stopped and faced her. "They said they were going to do a Senator, right?"

Bonnie nodded. Those were the words she remembered very clearly.

"Who knows," Craig said, "maybe they were talking about getting a hooker for a senator and accident was how they were describing it."

Bonnie laughed, but she knew Craig was right. A single part of an overheard conversation could mean so many things, they didn't dare jump to too many conclusions. Especially the conclusions they were both jumping to.

"So what do we do now?" she asked.

"I suppose we should take things one step at a time," Craig said. He glanced at the clock on the stand beside the bed. "It's only a little after ten. Let's find out if there's a Senator registered here."

"And just how do you plan to do that?" she asked. "I doubt anyone is just going to tell you."

"You would be surprised," he said, smiling. He picked up the phone and punched a button.

Bonnie lay back on the bed. She could still feel the tingle from the fun they had had on the fairway. It had been intense, that much was for sure. And even more startling that they could fall asleep nude like that in the middle of a fairway afterwards. The thought made her smile.

If she had her way, there were going to a few more encounters just like that one before this weekend was over.

As soon as they got all this stuff settled.

"Front desk?" Craig asked. Then after a moment he said casually, as if he said the words every day, "Would you connect me to the Senator's head-of-staff, please?"

"Good thinking," she whispered, smiling at her husband. "but it won't work." Craig was such a good detective, she knew. And he had ways of getting information that most people would never think of. But a stranger didn't just go calling a hotel front desk and ask if a United States Senator was staying there. It didn't work that way. Important people had layers between themselves and the regular public. Protective and necessary layers because of all the nut cases in the world.

Of course, Craig hadn't asked to talk to a Senator, but instead he had asked for the Senator's head-of-staff. That detail might make all the difference.

"I'm being connected," he said, his eyes suddenly full of worry. He was clearly as surprised as she was, both at his idea working, and the fact that there was a Senator staying here.

"Oh, shit," she said, suddenly remembering why Craig was making the call. "There is a Senator here. Now what are we going to do?"

He held his hand up. "Yes, hello, uh... Senator Knight," Craig said, giving her the wide-eyed shock look.

Craig was actually talking to Senator Knight! Bonnie thought her stomach was going to jump out of her body. Senator Knight from California was one of the more powerful Senator's in all of Washington. What was he doing here? And what was he doing answering his own damned phone?

Craig went on, clearly deciding to tell the truth as he went. "My name is Detective Craig Frakes from Seattle. I'm sorry to bother you, but my wife and I overheard a conversation this evening that I think we should relay to you and your security staff, if you have a few moments."

Bonnie watched as Craig listened to the Senator. Then he said, "I don't honestly know how important it is, Senator. I suspect you would be the best one to judge that."

Craig nodded, then said, "Yes, sir. From Seattle. I can give you some names to call to check on who we are."

There was another long pause then Craig finished with, "Thank you, Senator, we'll be right up."

He hung up, then turned and smiled at her. "Better comb the grass out of your hair. We're about to meet Senator Knight."

"Wonderful," she said, shaking her head as she jumped to her feet and headed for the bathroom. "He's going to think we're a couple of nutballs, you know that, don't you?"

Craig laughed. "More than likely. But at least our consciences will be clear. He can decide to do what he wants with the information we heard."

He followed her into the bathroom as she grabbed a comb from their travel kit and started to brush the dried grass from her hair. She looked ruffled, and she doubted she was going to change that much in the few moments they had.

Craig reached under her arm and cupped her right breast, giving it a light squeeze. "Just checking to make sure they got put back into the right place."

She smiled at him. "Looks who's talking." She pointed at the lump in the front of his pants. "You might want to take your underwear out of your pocket. We don't want the Senator getting wrong ideas."

Craig laughed and pulled his underwear out and tossed them at the suitcase.

"We better take our badges with us," she said, putting the comb down and grabbing her purse, even though it didn't go with her shorts and blouse. "If I were the Senator's people, I'd damned well want to see them."

"Good thinking," Craig said, moving to dig his out of his suitcase. Bonnie knew that when traveling he never liked to carry it. He figured it would get him in more trouble than it was worth. But this time was different.

"And one more thing we might want to think about before we go up there," she said.

"And that is?" Craig asked as he stuffed his badge in his back pocket.

"What happens if one of the Senator's people is one of the people we overheard?"

"Shit," Craig said softly. He had clearly not thought about that possibility. "Would you recognize either voice?"

"Easily," she said. She doubted she would ever forget those two voices.

He nodded. "I think I would too. We're just going to have to chance it. And play it by ear if one of them is there."

She didn't much like playing a situation like this "by ear," but it seemed they had no choice.

Five minutes later they were on the top floor knocking on Senator Knight's door. Bonnie could feel the knot grow in her stomach as they waited. This was just plain crazy. How did they go from making love on a fairway to talking to a powerful United States Senator in the space of an hour? This was turning out to be one really strange vacation, and they hadn't even gotten through the first evening yet.

A young-looking man that Bonnie guessed to be no more than twenty-five, opened the door and nodded. "Identification please?"

Bonnie sighed at the sound of his voice. The young man clearly was not one of the men they had heard. She could tell Craig knew that as well.

Bonnie retrieved her badge from her purse while Craig showed his.

There was a moment of uneasy tension as the man studied both badges. "Seems fine," he said, nodding and handing the badges back. Then he extended his hand, smiling. "Steve Parsons, Senator Knight's assistant. Come on in."

Craig shook his hand, then Bonnie did. Parsons' hand felt firm and warm, and his smile was winning without being too patronizing. Bonnie liked this guy at first glance. More than likely it was that skill that had gotten him the job with a powerful senator at such a young age.

"Sorry to bother you and the Senator like this," Craig said as Parsons led them into the massive suite, "but we felt we had to tell someone what we heard."

"No problem," Parson's said. "We were just finishing up some paperwork before the weekend golf tournament. You can never get away from the stuff."

"I know how that feels," Craig said.

Bonnie got into the main area of the suite and simply stopped and stared. She had thought their room to be wonderful, but now it seemed much more like a regular hotel room. This suite clearly had numerous bedrooms and a massive living room and kitchen, all decorated in the soft earth and wood tones. The square footage was clearly more than their entire home.

"You sure got me intrigued," a voice came from around the corner in the kitchen. It also wasn't one of the voices on the path.

A moment later a refrigerator door closed and Senator Knight stepped toward them. He was holding a can of soda and wearing golf slacks and a polo shirt. He was also barefoot.

Bonnie was taken aback at the man's presence. His full head of gray hair seemed to shimmer and his smile filled the room. He extended his hand to her first. "I'm Darren Knight," he said, his voice firm.

Bonnie shook his firm hand and returned his smile. "Bonnie Stanley," she said. "And this is my husband Craig Frakes."

"Pleased to meet you, Senator," Craig said.

"Likewise, Detective," the Senator said, indicating they should take a seat. "And just so you know, on your way up here Parsons there called Seattle to make sure you two are who you say you are. You got glowing recommendations all around."

"Nice to know," Bonnie said.

"So what's this all about?" the Senator asked as he dropped down into one of the big chairs. Parsons took the other, leaving the massive couch to Craig and Bonnie.

Bonnie sat back, leaving Craig to sit on the edge of the couch and do the talking.

Craig explained that he and Bonnie had gone out for a walk and decided to sit behind a rock near the cart path to watch the stars.

At that Senator Knight gave her a smile. Bonnie could feel her face redden slightly. She had no doubt the Senator knew what they had been doing, but had the good taste to say nothing.

"We heard two voices coming down the path from the hotel," Craig said. "Men's voices."

"And they were talking about me?" Senator Knight asked.

"I honestly don't know," Craig said. "Let me see if I can tell you word-for-word what we heard."

Bonnie listened as Craig went on to tell the Senator almost exactly the conversation they had heard. She doubted she could have relayed the words so accurately, but that was part of what Craig did every day.

When he had finished, Senator Knight turned to Bonnie. "Is this what you heard as well?" he asked. "Did your husband miss anything?"

She liked the man's question. He was being careful and making sure everything was clear. "I don't think he missed a word, Senator," Bonnie said. "And he added nothing."

The Senator nodded. "They didn't know you were there?"

"They didn't," Craig said. "And we made sure they were long gone before we moved. We went back to our room. We didn't know of any senator near here, so I called the desk, asking to be put through to someone on the Senator's staff, to see if there was even a senator here. They connected me to you."

"They did?" Parsons said, shaking his head. "That will change."

Bonnie smiled at the guy. Clearly someone in the hotel had screwed up and Parsons was going to make sure it didn't happen again.

Craig went on. "Can you see why we thought you and your security people should be notified?"

The Senator laughed. "Sure, but I'm afraid you are looking at my security team and my entire traveling staff."

Parsons sort of half-waved at Bonnie's stunned look.

Bonnie was shocked. She didn't know why, but she expected someone as important as Senator Knight to have security around him.

"Oh," Craig said, glancing at Parsons who only looked worried in return.

You know," the Senator said, laughing, "I get threats and hate mail all the time in my line of work. Almost all of them turn out to be nut cases. Harmless fools who think that threatening a Senator will get something done."

"Has anyone threatened you here?" Bonnie asked, not really believing that the Senator wasn't worried.

"Nope," the Senator said. "Just here to play a few days golf in this charity tournament on my way back to Washington."

"Senator," Craig said, "I also deal with nut cases every day. And I don't think this is one time that should be taken lightly."

"I agree," Parsons said.

The Senator looked at Bonnie.

She nodded. "This sounded very serious. And since it is not something you knew about, or two of your staff speaking in a code, we have to assume the two men's words meant what we thought."

"Is there any kind of government protection you could get?" Craig asked.

The Senator laughed, his smile filling the room. Bonnie had never seen someone so assured and comfortable in such an odd situation.

"I'm afraid there isn't much," the Senator said.

"And really nothing that could help us this weekend," Parsons said. "The Capital security is geared to function in Washington."

"How about the Secret Service?" Bonnie asked. "Or maybe the FBI?"

The Senator shook his head. "Mostly the Secret Service is only for the President and past Presidents, vice Presidents, top White House Staff, Cabinet members, and others in direct line of succession to the Presidency. That bunch keeps them more than busy."

"We should call the local FBI," Parsons said, nodding to Bonnie.

She smiled back. She knew there had to be some branch of government who could help protect a Senator.

The Senator nodded and looked at Craig. "You don't mind telling the FBI what you heard?"

"Not at all," Craig said. "There's also an ex-Seattle cop working as a detective in the Scottsdale police force. I could give him a call as well."

Before the Senator could object, Parsons said, "I think that would be a good idea, Detective."

The Senator smiled at his assistant. "Just don't think of canceling me out of this golf tournament. I've been looking forward to this for a month."

"So have we," Bonnie said. And if she had her way, this problem wasn't going to get in the way of either the golf tournament or their vacation.

CHAPTER FIVE

Friday, April 7th
10:39 p.m.

THE HEAT HAD been almost too much for Steph Baines to bear. The men with weapons had led her out of her apartment and into the back of an older panel van. The windows in the back doors had been covered and there was a partition between the cargo area and the front seats that had no door or window in it.

When the van's doors were closed, two of the masked men had tied her up and put her on the metal floor in the back of the van. Her feet were tied with a twine that cut into the flesh around her ankles and her hands were yanked behind her back and tied with a softer rope.

Then they had left, shutting and clearly latching the van door. Then she had heard them climb into the front of the van and start the engine. She could sit up, but not comfortably. Every corner the van took had sent her sprawling on the metal floor. Finally, after twenty minutes of trying to stay sitting, she had given up and remained on her side, her feet braced against the side of the van to help stop her from sliding around.

This was all the worst nightmare she could have ever imagined. She had simply taken the morning off from school to help Danny get ready for the weekend golf tournament. During the entire drive all she could think was wonder why had they picked her?

And what did they have in mind for her?

She had tried not to think about that second question, mostly without luck. Everything her imagination had come up with was too horrible to even consider.

For an eternity the van had seemed to drive on a freeway. She had moved around enough to find a half-comfortable position. The heat also kept getting worse and worse and sweat ended up coating her skin and streaking her with the dirt and dust from the floor.

During one smooth stretch of road she had managed to move over to a sharp edge sticking out of one wall and work the rope around her wrists against it. But before she could get it cut, the van had jerked and she had cut herself. Her blood had felt warm dripping off her fingers and down her back. She had had no idea how bad she had sliced herself, but she hadn't tried cutting the rope again. After a few minutes the bleeding had stopped. She had no doubt that if she had cut herself deeply, she would have bled to death before any of the men even noticed or cared.

Finally, after a bunch of turns and starts and stops, the van had stopped and the engine had shut off.

No one had opened the door to the van.

No one had come to give her water.

The sun had just baked the van into an oven.

For an eternity she had just sat there until finally she lay down and let the heat take her.

The next thing she knew a man was saying, "Here, drink this."

She felt wonderful, cool water pour over her lips and she had managed to choke a little of it down.

"Stupid idiots," the man said. "They almost killed you."

She had let more of the water in and swallowed, then had opened her eyes enough to see the unmasked man who had kidnapped her.

The guy smiled. "Good, glad you're still with us lady." He turned to someone beside her that she couldn't see. "Take her inside and get her situated in the second bathroom."

She had felt hands roughly pick her up and carry her just before the world left her again.

Now the darkness seemed to push back one more time as she came to again. This time she was lying on a soft rug on a small bathroom floor. Her hands and feet were untied and a bright light was on over the bathroom mirror.

Slowly, fighting the dizziness, she pulled herself up to a kneeling position and turned on the water in the sink. Using her hand as a cup she managed to drink a little more before slumping back to the wonderful coolness of the floor.

She just knew that in a short time she'd wake up beside Danny and this would all be a nightmare, that he would hold her and help her get over.

All she had to do was wake up.

She lay on her back, staring up at the bathroom light, waiting.

But the nightmare just wouldn't go away.

CHAPTER SIX

Friday, April 7th
11:12 p.m.

IT HAD TAKEN Parsons two phone calls to get an FBI agent on the way.

Craig had used a second line at the same time to get in touch with Detective Hagar Daniels, formally of Seattle, now part of the Scottsdale police force.

Twenty minutes later Hagar had arrived at the Senator's suite, followed in less than a minute by John Maxwell of the FBI.

Bonnie remembered Hagar from his time in the Seattle force. He was a big man, well over six-four, with broad shoulders, a small gut, and a sense of humor that seemed almost too dry. He arrived wearing white Bermuda shorts, a golf shirt, and sandals.

Maxwell, from the FBI, was even more casually dressed in jeans, a Grateful Dead tee-shirt, and a Phoenix Suns baseball cap.

He stood about Craig's height at six foot, and was trim and clearly in shape. His most striking feature were his deep blue eyes that Bonnie felt saw everything.

Maxwell and Hagar clearly knew each other, and liked each other. Bonnie had a sneaking hunch they had worked together a number of times before and didn't have the rivalry that sometimes happened between local cops and the FBI.

After all the introductions and badge exchanges were finished, the Senator had the two new arrivals join them in the large living room area of the suite and then had Craig relay exactly, word-for-word, what he and Bonnie had heard.

Bonnie was again amazed at how exact he got everything. There were times her husband impressed her and this was one of them.

After Craig had finished with the story and how he had informed the Senator, Hagar whistled softly. Then he said, "No wonder you called us."

Maxwell faced the Senator. "You don't have any friends or co-workers here with you besides Mr. Parsons?"

Bonnie liked the question. It was along the same lines that she and Craig had first thought might be a possibility.

"I sure don't," Senator Knight said. "It's just the two of us. I seldom travel with anyone else, do I?"

Parsons nodded his agreement, but said nothing.

"No meetings planned this weekend?" Maxwell asked.

"Just with my putter and thirty-six holes of golf," the Senator said, laughing.

"One more question," Maxwell said. "Has any person in this area threatened you lately?"

The Senator looked at his assistant. "I never read those kind of letters," he said. "You know of anyone?"

Parsons shook his head slowly. "All the threatening letters are back in the office in Washington. I don't remember any lately from this area, but I could have that checked in the morning."

"I think getting someone to do it tonight might be a better idea," Craig said.

Bonnie completely agreed. The morning might be too late.

Maxwell nodded. "I agree. I'll have someone from the Washington bureau meet one of your staff members tonight to go through the letters."

Parsons laughed. "Jenny, the Senator's secretary, isn't going to be happy."

The Senator joined in. "Got that right. Monday in the office is going to be hell."

"Better than no Monday," Maxwell said seriously.

Bonnie agreed, but the Senator just waved a hand dismissing the somber tone. It seemed that even though this was his life they were all worried about, the Senator wasn't going to let it bother him. He was here to have fun and damned if he was going to let anything like someone threatening his life get in the way.

But if he wasn't going to be worried, Bonnie knew that the rest of them had to worry for him. Which meant they had to stay close to him, and during a golf tournament, that wasn't going to be easy to do.

"Senator?" Bonnie said, "who are you planning on playing with in the tournament tomorrow?"

"They got me scheduled with a young, hot pro from the Sedona area," the Senator said. "Beyond that, I don't have any idea."

"Well," Bonnie said, smiling at the Senator, "Craig and I are here to play as well. Mind if we join you?"

"Dear Ms. Stanley," the Senator said, "that would be my pleasure."

Bonnie could feel herself blushing slightly again. Why the Senator did that to her she had no idea. Out of the corner of her eye she could see both Craig and Hagar nodding, clearly agreeing with the idea of she and Craig playing the round with the Senator.

"Well, people," the Senator said, standing. "My tee time is at eight-forty-six in the morning, and I plan on getting a good night's sleep. Thank you all for your concern."

With that he headed into the bedroom to the right of the living area and shut the door.

His exit felt sudden to Bonnie, but correct. There was nothing more he could do now, so he left the planning in the hands of the people who knew what they were doing. He was clearly a person who knew how to delegate and was used to doing just that.

One hour later, Craig and Bonnie left, heading for their room.

Bonnie was tired, and they had to be up early for the tee time, but she knew there was no chance she could get to sleep at once after all that had happened. She wasn't sure she was going to get much sleep the entire night.

An FBI agent was standing at the end of the corridor as they headed for the elevator, clearly on post for the evening. He nodded good night to them. Maxwell was efficient and already covering the Senator. That made Bonnie feel a lot better.

Bonnie had been impressed with both Maxwell and Hagar. After the Senator went to bed, the four of them had planned what measures were needed to guard someone on a rocky, desert golf course. Much of the close-in duty was going to fall on Bonnie and Craig's shoulders, and Hagar was going to furnish them both with side-arms tomorrow to carry in their golf bags just in case. Maxwell would ride in a cart along with the group as well, with his people and Hagar's people set up along the course in an unobtrusive manner.

Everything was being done that the four of them could think to do. Even Parsons seemed satisfied with the plans after getting off the phone with the Senator's staff in Washington.

The only thing they couldn't figure out was who would want the Senator hurt, and who would pay big money, as the two men on the path had said, to have it done? Both Hagar and Maxwell said they would have full teams working that end of the problem.

Bonnie and Craig rode in silence down the elevator and to their room.

As Craig opened the door she said, "Seems we're not going to get away from work after all."

"Yeah, I'm afraid we were in the wrong place at the wrong time."

Bonnie moved inside and Craig let the door close behind them, locking the safely bolt. Then he turned and she put her arms around his neck, kissing him lightly. "I thought it was fun out there on that fairway. Didn't you?"

Craig pulled her close and kissed her hard. Then he pulled back and smiled. "Lots of fun."

"Worth all these problems?"

He pretended to be serious. "Sex with you is never a problem and always worth it."

"Ahh, the right thing for a husband to say," she said, kissing him again. "The exact right thing."

CHAPTER SEVEN

Saturday, April 8th
8:04 a.m.

AT SLIGHTLY AFTER eight in the morning, the desert sun was still a good hour from completely taking the chill off the morning air. Craig hadn't bothered to grab a jacket when he left the room for breakfast, but after walking from the clubhouse to the cart area, he wished he had. He was only wearing golf slacks and a short-sleeved shirt. He knew that by noon he was going to be too warm, but right now he was darned cold.

No doubt Bonnie was as well. She had on a pair of tight white shorts and a thin, see-through blouse with a white halter-top underneath. It was an outfit that was sure to drive the Senator to distraction by the time the round was over. Watching that wonderful body in those tight shorts wasn't going to exactly help keep Craig's mind on the game either.

Right now, because of the cold, Bonnie's nipples were clearly visible as sharp bumps standing out against the halter-top and blouse. She had her arms crossed under her breasts for warmth, not covering anything.

About a hundred identical golf carts were all lined two abreast along a wide area of concrete to one side of the clubhouse, ready to go for the tournament. Each pair of carts had white pieces of paper with different tee-times on the steering wheels.

Craig and Bonnie moved down the line until they found their 8:46 time that Hagar had arranged last night with the tournament staff. Their golf clubs were already loaded into two carts, Bonnie's in the cart with Senator Knight's bag and Craig's beside a large black bag that had the word Titleist covering one side. Clearly Craig was riding with the pro and Bonnie was riding with the Senator.

Craig wasn't too sure if he liked the idea of Bonnie being that close to the possible target of an assassin, but he couldn't think of any logical reason to change the pairing.

There were a lot of people coming and going from around the carts and bags, but there was no sign of the Senator or Maxwell or Hagar.

"Damn, it's cold out here," Bonnie said, grabbing her visor from the front pocket of her bag.

"Wait an hour and that will change," Craig said.

"I may be frozen stiff in an hour," Bonnie said.

"Parts of you already are stiff," Craig said, glancing down at where her nipples were trying to break free from her blouse.

She smacked his arm in mock anger, but he could tell she was enjoying the attention.

"Excuse me, Detective Craig and Officer Stanley," a man said, moving up beside them.

Craig glanced up as a guy in blue slacks and white jacket approached. He was either FBI, one of Hagar's men, or one of the golf pros. Craig would bet a month's salary on FBI.

"I'm Agent Howard," the man said. "The Senator is on the driving range. He told me to tell you to bring both the carts."

"Thanks," Craig said.

"One more thing," Agent Howard said, moving in so his voice could only be heard by Craig and Bonnie. "In the outside pocket of both your bags are loaded weapons. Detective Hagar wanted me to make sure you knew where they were."

Craig nodded and turned to his bag. He unzipped the outside pocket just enough to see the handle of the police special stuffed down in his rain gear. It was the exact same model as his gun back in Seattle.

"Got it," he said, zipping up the pocket and turning back to the agent.

Bonnie looked up from her bag, a grim look on her face. "Should work fine if I have to use it."

"Let's hope we don't," Agent Howard said.

"Couldn't agree more," Craig said. "Thanks."

Agent Howard turned and moved away from them, walking down the row of carts as if he belonged here.

"I wonder how many other FBI and Scottsdale police are around," Bonnie said.

"More than we're going to spot," Craig said, "if they are doing their job."

Craig moved over and sat down on the cold cart seat. "Follow me."

Bonnie dropped down behind the wheel of the other cart, then said, "Holy shit, that's cold."

Craig laughed.

"What's so funny?" Bonnie asked, glaring at him. "I didn't come to Arizona to freeze my ass off."

"Trust me," Craig said, turning the cart out of line and starting toward the driving range. "You'll be wishing for a cold seat in two hours."

He couldn't hear Bonnie's answer.

The path to the driving range was at least four hundred yards of winding pavement that led up over the top of a rock bluff and down into a steep valley hidden from the clubhouse. The wind in his face was biting-cold, and he drove with only one hand, keeping the other under his leg for some warmth.

As he cleared the top of the ridge, he was colder than he could remember being in a long, long time.

The driving range spread out below him, filling a massive open area of green that sloped down the floor of the rock-sided valley. Colored flags were placed at different distances from the teeing area.

Twenty or so people were scattered over the teeing area that looked like it could hold at least fifty people hitting balls at the same time. Each player had his or her own area marked by a metal stand to lean clubs against, a small rock, and a shining pile of red-striped golf balls. Craig loved the free driving-range balls when coming to the desert. Back in the Northwest, driving-range balls were normally sold by the bucket. Down here they just piled them up for every player to use as many as they wanted.

Maxwell was sitting in a cart just off the path on the far side of the range and Hagar and two others were talking off to the right side.

Craig waved at them and then looked around for the Senator. He was at the far left side of the range, his back to the hill and Maxwell. It was the easiest spot to guard in the entire area.

Craig took the cart down the path, parking it directly behind the Senator. Bonnie pulled up behind him, clearly even colder than she had been back at the clubhouse. Her fingers looked white as she blew on them, and Craig could swear her teeth were chattering.

"Are we having fun yet?" he asked, smiling at her.

She only glared at him and moved around to get some clubs out of her bag.

"Not yet, huh?" he said, laughing as he grabbed a few clubs and headed to a pile of balls. The Senator glanced up and said, "Good morning."

"Morning, sir," Craig said.

The Senator was wearing green Bermuda shorts and a Hawaiian shirt that would clash with anything. He had on white socks and black golf shoes. Anyone trying to take a shot at this guy would be laughing too hard to shoot straight.

"Good morning, Senator," Bonnie said, walking up and standing behind him. "You look colorful this morning."

The Senator laughed. "A natural politician. I knew I liked you for more than your fantastic looks."

Bonnie blushed. Craig could very seldom get that kind of reaction out of her, yet the Senator seemed to be able to do it at will.

The Senator pointed to a man two spots over hitting balls with a fluid golf swing. "Craig, Bonnie, that is Danny Baines. From Sedona."

Danny turned and stepped toward them, his hand outstretched, a smile filling his face. Danny had to be all of twenty, if that. He had the kind of face that Craig figured women loved. Sort of a cross between Paul McCartney and Paul Newman. But there was something about him that bothered Craig almost instantly. And he wasn't sure what it was.

"Nice to meet you both," the kid-pro said. "Looking forward to our round."

"Yeah," Bonnie said. "Me too."

After she had shaken the kid's hand, she turned and gave Craig the eyebrows-up, wide-eyed look. He wasn't sure if that meant she thought the kid was hot, or if it meant she was feeling the same way he was. He'd ask her when he got a chance.

Thirty minutes later, Craig rolled his drive off the first tee, the Senator hit his drive into a large pile of rocks to the left of the fairway, and Bonnie and the pro hit the fairway. It was a good indication of how the day would go.

Chapter Eight

BONNIE FIGURED SHE had gotten the best deal, riding with the Senator. He was charming, laughed easily, and was determined to have fun, no matter how bad his golf game was. And it was bad, plain and simple.

The first hole he had managed a nine from the rocks, and except for a bogey four on a short par three, that was his best score. The good thing was that he didn't take much time over any single shot. He just walked up to it, took his stance and hit it, often sideways and never very far.

The young pro was another matter. He was the silent type who had had it two under par by the end of the first nine, and took lots of time over each shot. However, he had taken so many fewer shots than the rest of them, it didn't really slow them down at all.

Also the kid hadn't said much more than "Nice shot!" or "Your turn," the entire morning. Bonnie hadn't been able to figure out what bothered her about the kid, but one thing for sure, he had a beautiful golf swing.

The Senator had Bonnie so relaxed with his jokes and friendly patter that by the second hole, even with the distraction of always looking around, always being aware of any danger, she had played well.

Far better than Craig had, that was for sure.

The temperature had finally warmed up enough to be comfortable by the third hole, and by the time they had reached the tenth hole it was warm. By the scenic sixteenth hole tee box on the back nine, it was just plain hot.

The sixteenth was a fairly long par three, with the tee boxes for the hole carved out of the side of a large hill, and the green a good hundred feet below them across a deep rock canyon. The group in front of them was still on the green, so Bonnie climbed up the dirt and wood steps to get on the highest tee box. Maxwell and another FBI agent were already up there, off to one side, scanning the surrounding area.

The light wind blew at her blouse and hair, cooling her as she looked around. The view was just spectacular. Where she stood was by far the highest place on the golf course, and from there she could see out over Scottsdale and Phoenix.

"Wow," Senator Knight said, moving up to stand beside her. "This is a sight."

"I didn't know Senators were prone to understatement," Bonnie said.

The Senator laughed. "The spectacular view took my words away."

"That's better," Bonnie said, smiling at him.

Below them the cart path wound back and forth, switchback after switchback, down the almost cliff-steep side of the mountain between the tee box and the green.

And there were dirt footpaths in the rocks and scrub brush leading down into the canyon where golfers had climbed down to search for balls. If she hit one down in there, she wasn't going down looking for it, that was for sure. Too many snake-warning signs around this course for her tastes. Since she saw the first sign back on the fifth hole, she hadn't gotten off the cart path or fairway without a club in her hand.

Two of Hagar's men stood on the hill on the far side of the hole, waiting. She could imagine how boring the day had been for them. Climbing around in the rocks and desert, watching four people play golf.

Thank heavens that was all that had happened so far.

Craig moved up beside her and whispered in her ear. "What do you say we come back up here tonight?"

"And do what?" she whispered back, teasing him.

"An encore performance," he said, just loud enough for her to hear.

"Sex on the top of a mountain," she whispered. "I like that idea. As long as you carry me up here."

Craig laughed and said loud enough for the Senator to hear. "It might just be worth it."

The Senator gave her a raised-eyebrow look and Bonnie could feel herself blush again.

Then he said, smiling at her, "Green's open."

What seemed like an outrageous distance below her the foursome in front of them cleared the green and Danny moved to the tee.

His shot sailed into the air and then seemed to drop forever. At first she thought it was going to be so far over the green that it might land on one of Hagar's men on the far hillside. But finally the ball dropped about twenty paces short of the pin, bounced once and stopped. In all the years she had played golf, she had never been on a hole like this.

She hit two balls into the canyon before she declared she was done and was going to drop a ball up by the green. This might be the most spectacular vista in the desert, but it was also one impossible golf hole.

Craig managed to hit one over the canyon, landing it on the right of the green and they all cheered him like he'd just hit a home run. As far as Bonnie was concerned, that was his best shot of the day.

Even Maxwell applauded.

The Senator rolled a shot off the end of the tee box. They all watched as the ball bounced, clattered, and fell like a pinball gone crazy down the rocky slope. It bounced twice on the cart path, once about twenty feet below the tee box, and a second time somewhere even with the green about three switchbacks down. The ball finally disappeared into the canyon in front of the green.

The Senator glanced over at Danny. "I think that ball went four hundred yards at least, if you count every bounce."

Danny nodded. "Thank your lucky stars it didn't get stuck somewhere on that cliff. You would have had to try to hit it."

"Not in this lifetime," the Senator said, glancing down the steep slope.

The Senator tried one more shot—this time flying his ball into the canyon—and decided Bonnie's idea of dropping one on the other side was the best policy. Everyone agreed.

Bonnie climbed into the cart beside the Senator and stared at the sign twenty feet in front of them.

WARNING!
STEEP DOWNGRADE!
SLOW!
USE BRAKES!

Thank heavens the Senator took the warning to heart. The hole was no more than one hundred and seventy yards as the crow flies, but the cart path down that cliff face had to be five times that long. And very, very narrow and steep. She was sweating more from the fear than the heat by the time they reached the flat bridge over the canyon in front of the green.

The Senator's knuckles were white on the steering wheel.

It was a golf hole, and a golf cart ride she would never forget.

They made it the rest of the way through the round without problems, and the Senator agreed to meet them in the bar for drinks after a shower and change of clothes.

"You don't mind, do you Senator," Craig asked, "if we play with you again tomorrow?"

Hagar and Maxwell were both standing close by and both nodded their agreement with the idea.

"Sounds fine with me," the Senator said. "As long as Bonnie wears those white shorts again."

For the fifth or sixth time, Bonnie blushed. Why he could do that to her, she didn't know.

"She has another pair that is even tighter," Craig said, winking at the Senator.

Bonnie punched him in the arm as the Senator laughed. She did have a tighter pair, and now she planned on wearing them for sure.

"Then I look forward to the round," the Senator said. "I'll meet you in the bar in an hour."

Bonnie glanced at her watch. It was a little after two in the afternoon. A shower sounded perfect to help cool down and rinse off a layer of suntan lotion.

"Sounds great," Craig said.

"Drinks and dinner are on me," the Senator said. "For all of you. No arguments." He glanced at Maxwell and Hagar, who both nodded, then at Bonnie.

"It sounds like a wonderful time," she said.

"Good. An hour then." He turned and headed up into the hotel.

Maxwell moved with him and Bonnie had no doubt there were other FBI agents working ahead of the Senator. She really liked the guy, even though he made her blush with the slightest look. She was glad they were doing everything in their power to make sure nothing happened to him.

So far all was well. But there was still the rest of the afternoon and tonight.

And all of tomorrow.

CHAPTER NINE

Saturday, April 8th
9:07 p.m.

AFTER A QUICK shower in the strange waterfall tub, Craig had ended up having two rum and cokes in the bar. Those drinks, combined with a lot of laugher and jokes, had stretched over two hours. It had been almost six by the time they finally went into the restaurant for dinner, and Craig had been famished.

Bonnie had only had one drink and a lot of water and she whispered to him as they walked into the restaurant that she was so hungry, she was about to eat the bar napkins.

Parsons, Hagar and Maxwell had joined them in the bar. Parsons said he didn't drink and Hagar and Maxwell had both stuck to Diet Cokes since they were on duty. Craig could see a few other detectives and agents stationed around the bar and restaurant.

The food had turned out to be even better than Craig would have expected, and his expectations were high in this beautiful resort. He had had a perfectly cooked New York steak, while Bonnie had lamb.

The food was so good, Craig just didn't want to stop eating.

Finally, at nine the Senator excused himself, saying it was time to get back to his room, do a little work, and get some sleep, since their tee time in the morning was 8:15.

Maxwell and Hagar left the table with the Senator and Parsons, leaving only Craig and Bonnie. As she pushed away the last few bites of her raspberry-covered cheesecake she moaned.

"Full?"

"Stuffed like a turkey at Thanksgiving," she said, sipping on her coffee.

"Before or after roasting?"

She touched her suntanned arm. "After, clearly."

"So what do you say we go for a walk?" Craig asked. "It's getting dark."

"To walk off the dinner, or did you have something else in mind?'

"Maybe both," he said.

"Perfect."

Hand in hand they strolled out of the restaurant and through the lobby. Not only was the restaurant and bar still busy, but so was the central area of the massive hotel. Craig figured at least a hundred people milled around in the vast wood and stone space, talking and laughing and generally enjoying the party atmosphere of the charity golf tournament. Even with the fear for the Senator, he was enjoying himself as well.

And, it seemed, Bonnie was too.

"Let's go out this way," Craig said, pulling Bonnie through the lobby away from the front door and down a wide hallway that led to the pro shop area. He knew there was another door there that went out toward the back nine.

Last night they had gone out the front and ended up on the second hole. When they went past the spot this morning Bonnie had pointed out to the Senator where they were sitting when they overheard the men. The Senator's only comment was, "It looks like a nice private spot to me."

Bonnie had blushed.

Craig was enjoying the fact that the Senator could make her blush with a simple comment.

The Pro Shop was closed, so Craig led Bonnie down the wide staircase to an outside door between the entrances to the locker rooms. Where the carts had been lined up early that morning was an empty expanse of concrete. To the left Craig could see a large, open door behind a massive boulder. It looked as if it led down into what was clearly a cart storage area under the hotel.

There was no one around. Compared to the massive number of people just a short distance away in the lobby and restaurant area, it felt odd to be alone.

Bonnie ambled toward the open door. "I wonder how many carts a place like this has?"

"They have two courses here," he said. "It has to be a lot. A couple hundred at least." He followed her down the ramp around the rock and into a massive, low-ceilinged garage area.

"Try four or five hundred," Bonnie said.

Craig stood in the door beside her, amazed at the expanse of lined up carts that seemed to almost vanish into the distance in the dim light. They were in perfect rows, with cords draping from the ceiling. Each cord was plugged into a cart in the center under the seat.

To Craig it looked like each was hooked into an umbilical cord.

The carts were all empty and cleaned, waiting, the clubs clearly off in a locked storage area somewhere.

Bonnie walked slowly down one aisle. Each cart was numbered, and that number matched a number painted on the concrete. It looked like something he'd seen in a bad science fiction movie: aliens waiting to be activated. And the dim light didn't help the image.

"I wonder what their power bill is like for all this," Bonnie said, pointing up at all the chargers on shelves along one ceiling beam.

Craig followed, not sure that they should be in there, but not stopping either.

Bonnie glanced over at Craig. "You remember what our cart numbers were today?"

"You and the Senator had 167 and Danny and I had 168," he said, surprised at himself for remembering. But since he and Danny had been following the Senator's cart all day, and the number to their cart was on the back right bumper, it had pretty much stuck in his mind.

They were walking along the carts with low eighties for numbers. Bonnie kept going, deeper into the dimly-lit room. He had no idea what she had in mind, but he followed anyway.

She led him between cart 104 and 105 over to the next row. Cart 167 was backed against the concrete wall five or six carts from the back of the room. Bonnie climbed in and patted the seat beside her.

"Just what are we doing?" Craig asked, sliding into the passenger seat.

"Shhh," she said softly. "Just listen."

The silence seemed to suddenly get louder than his own heartbeat as they sat there in the darkness. The light from the door they had come in was the only bright area. The rest of the massive garage was illuminated by dim nightlights scattered on support pillars. There was a faint hum that filled the air, more than likely coming from the chargers above each cart.

Nothing else.

Bonnie moved her hand to his lap and squeezed. Then she whispered, "Every time you climbed in the cart today I wanted to do that."

"Don't stop now," he whispered back.

Her hand worked over his crotch, rubbing him through his slacks, making him grow quickly hard.

"Nice," he whispered. "Very nice." He leaned into her and they kissed, long and hard, the taste of the cheesecake dessert covering her breath like a sweet mint.

He moved his hands up to her breasts, rubbing them through her blouse and bra. He felt like a high school kid again, out parking on a date, touching a girl's breasts through her blouse. Those nights were exciting and frustrating at the same time. He had loved the feeling and had always wished he could recapture it.

Now he was and it was great.

Excitement of being in a different place combined with sexual touching, all wrapped into the fear of getting caught. This weekend was going to be memorable for a number of things.

Bonnie seemed to be enjoying it just like his dates had back then. Actually, he was enjoying it more than he had in high school, since none of his dates had ever put her hand on his crotch like Bonnie was doing now.

They kissed again, long and hard and passionately. It seemed it had been years since the two of them had felt so passionate with each other. Craig knew right then they were going to have to take vacations much more often.

Bonnie started fumbling to unzip his pants and open his belt. He broke the kiss to help, but before he could get his belt undone the sound of something metal dropping echoed through the massive empty room.

Both Bonnie and Craig jerked away from each other to stare out through the carts. Craig thought his heart was going to jump right out of his chest from the shock. Across the massive garage, at least six rows over, Craig could see two men moving toward the door.

He couldn't see their faces, since their backs were mostly turned toward them, but one had short hair, the other wore a golf cap. Both looked to be about six foot, one had wider shoulders than the other.

As the two neared the door, one spoke, clearly loud enough for Bonnie and Craig to hear. "Man, you two need to get a room."

Then the two men were gone out the door and up the ramp.

Craig glanced at the shocked look on Bonnie's face. Instantly he knew she thought the same thing he did. That voice was one of the voices from last night.

"Come on," he said, jumping out of the cart and running down the aisle toward the door, making sure his zipper was up as he ran.

"We don't have our guns," Bonnie said from behind him.

Craig knew that. "I don't plan on stopping them. Just following."

At the large door he stopped and quickly peered around the corner. As he had expected, they were not in sight up the ramp. With Bonnie right behind him he ran up to the door into the clubhouse. There were two couples walking out near one of the putting greens, and a maintenance man working in the ground near a planter, but no sign of the two men.

"They must have gone inside," Bonnie said, pointing to the double doors that led past the pro shop and up the stairs.

Craig agreed. It was the only place they could have gone that quickly.

At a run they went back up the stairs, down the hall, and into the main lobby. There seemed to be even more people up here than there had when they left a half hour before.

He and Bonnie moved to one side and stood, scanning the people. Not a sign of the two men.

They had vanished.

"Damn," Bonnie said.

Craig couldn't agree more. "We need to inform Maxwell and Hagar. Let's head up to the Senator's floor."

"Just don't tell the Senator what we were doing," Bonnie said. "I get embarrassed enough around that man."

"Agreed," Craig said, smiling. "But we have to tell the others what the guy said."

"Damn, damn, damn," Bonnie said. "Caught parking in a golf cart inside a garage. How bad is that?"

"And with a married man as well," Craig said. "What's your husband going to say?"

"I hope he says rain check."

"Rain check."

Ten minutes later, with Hagar and Maxwell and two other FBI agents with them, they did a sweep through the hotel lobby, bar, and restaurant, looking for two men who matched the vague description of what Bonnie and Craig had seen. No luck at all, which just made Craig even that much more frustrated.

They all then went back down to the cart storage area. With Bonnie's help, they managed to figure out which row the two men had seemed to suddenly appear in. Hagar got one of the hotel security staff to turn up the lights and they searched the entire area without finding anything.

Maxwell pointed at a regular-sized door in the back wall near the end of the cart aisle they were searching. "Maybe they came out of there." Maxwell glanced at one of the hotel security guards. "Where's that lead?"

"Service area," the security guard said.

"We didn't hear a door open or close," Craig said. He glanced at Bonnie to make sure and she nodded her agreement.

"They might have already come through it when we came in," Bonnie said.

Maxwell nodded and moved to the door. It was locked, but the security guard quickly had it open. The door was the kind that could be opened from the inside even if locked so the two men could have easily come through it from the inside. Behind the door was a staircase leading upwards into a main floor service area of the hotel. And right across from where the staircase came out were three service elevators.

"It seems the two we are looking for know their way around this place," Bonnie said.

"I hope you have those guarded," Craig said, pointing at the service elevators.

"On the Senator's floor we do," Maxwell said. "But I'm beginning to think we may need to cover the floor below as well."

Craig could only agree.

CHAPTER TEN

Saturday, April 8th
10:19 p.m.

CHARLES ROBINS MOVED out onto his patio toward the man standing there. Never had the man returned in the middle of an assignment before. And never had the man called him on his personal, unlisted number to set up a meeting so late.

Charles had paced for the last two hours, waiting, coming up with a dozen things that could have gone wrong. Clearly the Senator had not met with his accident yet, so something had. The question was what?

And how serious was the problem?

Finally the man in the dark suit had appeared on the patio, smoking as always.

"So what has gone wrong?" Charles demanded.

"You tell me," the man said, his voice low and very mean. "The Senator has clearly been tipped that something might happen to him this weekend. Both the Scottsdale authorities and the FBI are staying very close to him. And he is playing with two cops from Seattle."

Charles felt as if someone had punched him in the stomach. "How? I said nothing to anyone but you."

"Are you sure?" the man asked, his voice seemingly on the edge of anger, barely controlled. His eyes were like two black holes in the darkness, unblinking and deadly.

"Of course I'm sure," Charles said, disgusted. "If Senator Knight makes that vote on Monday, I'm as good as broke and in prison. It would only be a matter of time. So why the hell would I tell anyone I'm trying to stop him?"

"Well, they have discovered the threat to the Senator in some fashion," the man said.

"But can you still do what needs to be done?"

The man nodded. "The Senator can still meet his date with an accident. But it will cost you a great deal more than before. And this will be our last meeting ever."

"How much more?" Charles demanded. The man's fee hadn't been small before this set-back.

The man laughed. "This is not a negotiation." He handed Charles a slip of paper.

Charles did not even give the man the satisfaction of looking down at the note.

"If the first amount specified is not in that off-shore numbered account by ten in the morning, the Senator will make his plane to Washington just fine."

"And if I put the money in the account and you do not carry through on your end of the deal?" Charles demanded, getting angrier and angrier.

"Then you do not have to pay the second, larger payment specified."

That made Charles glance down at the paper, but he could not read it in the dim light.

"And trust me," the man said, "if I carry through with my end of this and you do not pay the second amount, you will meet an accident far worse than what waits for the Senator. And far more painful."

"You are threatening me?" Charles demanded, stepping toward the man. Charles could not remember ever being so angry as to want to hit someone. But right now he was.

The man stood his ground, his dark eyes intense, his posture relaxed. "Of course I am."

Charles just stared at the man. This man was blackmailing him and there was nothing at all he could do about it. Charles was going to lose everything and the man knew it and was using that fact to extract everything he could.

"Think it over," the man said.

"How do I know you didn't make up this entire story about the FBI knowing there is a threat to the Senator?"

"You don't," the man said. "But it is the truth and there is no way to prove it to you."

Charles stared at the man. More than likely this guy had just been waiting for the right assignment from Charles to pull this blackmail stunt and then vanish. More than likely the man had done the same to other clients in the past and gotten away with it.

Well, he was going to get away with it again. Charles was desperate. Senator Knight had to be kept from that vote on Monday. There was no other choice.

"All right," Charles said. "The money will be in the account in the morning."

"It has been nice doing business with you," the man said, turning from Charles and starting across the patio.

"Just make sure it's done," Charles said.

"Oh, I will be successful," the man said without looking back. "You just make sure the payments are made and we can both live happily ever after."

With that the man walked down the path away from the patio and vanished into the night.

Charles turned and moved back into the light so that he could read the amounts on the paper. His stomach clamped up like the guy had punched him. $250,000 by ten in the morning. $750,000 within twelve hours of completion.

"Damn, damn, damn," he said, glancing around to see if the man was still in sight. That was a vast amount of money, yet possible. And the man he called Bill knew it. Its removal from his corporate accounts was going to be hard to hide, but better taking a chance with some missing money than having Knight vote on Monday.

He turned and headed for the office he kept here in his home. It was far past the time he would normally be in bed, but he knew without a doubt there would be no sleeping tonight. He had to figure a way to cover his tracks with the money.

And then spend the rest of the night worrying about the thousand things that might go wrong.

CHAPTER ELEVEN

Saturday, April 8th
11:30 p.m.

DANNY OPENED THE door for the man and stepped back into his hotel room. All day he had been simply walking through the motions. He had managed to play decent golf, but that had been mostly because he hadn't cared. He kept thinking about his wife. He couldn't imagine what they were doing to her, and yet he couldn't think of anything at all to do. If he told someone, they would kill her, he had no doubt. And he couldn't live with that.

But he was also starting to wonder if he could live with the Senator getting hurt.

"Nice to see you not bein' guarded, kid," the man said. "Lot of cops around here. You have anything to do with that?'

Danny suddenly felt his stomach clamp down into a tight knot. "No!" he said as firmly as he could. "I didn't say a word to anyone."

The guy nodded. "You sure about that?"

"You said you'd kill my wife," Danny said, staring into the dark eyes of the man. "Why would I chance that?"

The guy looked at him for a minute, then nodded. "Smart kid. I believe you. Besides, we've been keepin' an eye on you and I doubt you had a chance to tell anyone."

Danny felt the relief flood over him. "Can I talk to Steph?"

He had insisted that before he would do anything for them, he could talk to Steph every night. The kidnappers had agreed.

"Sure thing, kid," the guy said. He reached into his coat pocket and flipped Danny a cell phone. "Just hit redial."

He did as the man told him to do, then listened as it rang on the other end twice before Steph answered. "Danny?"

"Steph?" he said, the relief he felt flooding through him, making his knees weak and his eyes water.

"Are you all right, Danny?" she asked, her voice barely able to sustain the question.

"I'm fine," he managed to say. "How are they treating you?"

"They're keeping me locked in a bathroom," she said, "but they are feeding me and they haven't touched me."

"I love you," he said.

"I love you, too," she said.

The phone went dead.

He handed the cell phone back to the guy and he put it in his pocket. "You want to see that wonderful wife of yours again, you'll play along tomorrow."

"I'll do what you asked," Danny said.

"Good," the guy said, patting Danny on the shoulder as he headed for the door. "Then I'll see you tomorrow evening for the grand reunion with your wife."

Danny could only nod as the man opened the door, glanced in both directions, and then turned toward the elevators.

The door banged closed.

In all his life Danny had never felt so alone as he did right at that moment.

He stared at the closed door for the longest time before returning to the couch to try to watch television.

It was going to be another long, sleepless night.

A very lonely night.

CHAPTER TWELVE

Sunday, April 9th
6:00 a.m.

THE WAKE-UP CALL and the sun behind the pulled drapes came way, way too early, as far as Bonnie was concerned.

Craig grabbed the phone, listened for a moment, hung it back up, and then just lay beside her half-snoring, half-moaning.

She had the alarm clock set to go off ten minutes after the wake-up call, and if she had anything to do with it, she was going to make sure she used those ten minutes to get as much sleep as she could.

But the wake-up call stirred the memories of what had happened yesterday, and last night.

After the second trip to the cart shed and the discovery of the stairs up into the service area, she and Craig, along with Maxwell and Hagar, had spent two hours planning the protection of the Senator today. Hagar was going to bring in an extra three men, and Maxwell would also have extra men on duty, but he never said how many.

Bonnie never expected to meet any of them. More than likely, knowing how efficient Maxwell had been so far, those extra men would be posing as staff, or even playing in the group ahead of the Senator.

By the time midnight had come around, they had ways figured to keep the Senator completely covered from the moment he left his room to the moment he got on the plane headed for Washington. And as Maxwell assured them, even beyond. Even the plane he was due to fly on would be double-checked and all baggage scanned with special equipment.

Bonnie lay there, letting the conversations from last night go through her mind as Craig snored lightly beside her.

Maxwell had told them he had an idea as to who might want Senator Knight hurt. He had gone on to describe Charles Robins and the relationship between Robins and Senator Knight, including the vote on Monday in Washington in the Senator's committee that would surely cripple Robins' companies. The two men had never met, but were deadly enemies.

"Robins has enough at risk to hurt a United States Senator to stop it?" Bonnie had asked.

"More than enough," Maxwell had replied. "But we don't know for sure that he is behind anything. It could be literally anyone."

"Or that anything is even going to happen," Craig had reminded them. "We're still only acting on what we overheard by accident."

"Which is why we can only protect the Senator and see if anyone makes a move," Maxwell had said.

None of them liked that option, but there just wasn't any other plan as far as they could figure.

Now Bonnie lay in the bed waiting for the alarm to go off, listening to Craig snore, trying not to think about what the day might bring. There wasn't going to be any more sleeping for her, that was for sure. And if she couldn't sleep, Craig shouldn't be able to either.

She flicked off the alarm and rolled over to cuddle with him, putting her naked body the entire length of his back. His skin felt wonderful against hers, firm and smooth and warm.

She rubbed her hand over his unshaven face and then down his chest.

He moaned softly and then rolled toward her and onto his back.

She pushed the covers back so she could see what she was doing in the early morning light coming through the curtains. He didn't move or open his eyes.

She wondered how long he could stay still with her against him. As it turned out, not long. He nuzzled his chin into her neck, letting his unshaven stubble brush lightly against the sensitive area under her ear. The motion sent shivers down her spine and she pushed against him.

Their parking in the cart garage last night had been rudely interrupted and they had been too tired by the time they got back to the room to even think about finishing. But this morning was another matter.

Just the thought of what they had started last night in the cart got her even more excited.

She glanced at the clock. They didn't have much time if they were going to meet Hagar for breakfast.

But they had enough.

CHAPTER THIRTEEN

Sunday, April 9th
7:02 a.m.

BREAKFAST WITH HAGAR was quick, without much talk about what was going on that day with the Senator since they were in a public restaurant with a hundred other golfers. All Hagar had said was that his men were in place and ready. And that he just hoped like hell this was all going to be just a walk in the sun.

Craig agreed completely.

After freezing for the first hour yesterday, Craig brought a jacket and his gloves this morning. Bonnie had done the same, putting on a jacket and lined rain pants over her shorts, swearing she would never get as cold as she had been yesterday again.

Even with the jacket, Craig felt it was almost as cold. And when they reached their cart, they discovered they were riding together. The Senator's cart was already gone.

"I wonder why our cart assignments were switched?" Bonnie asked.

Craig only shrugged as he dropped down onto the cold seat behind the wheel. "Disappointed you have to ride with your husband?"

"When I can ride with a cute, older, and very powerful United States Senator?" Bonnie asked, smiling at him. "Of course."

She sat down next to him and put her hand in his lap. "But on the bright side," she said, "I can do this all day."

Craig laughed. "Just wait until it warms up and we get out behind some of those rocks on the back side. You'll see some groping then."

"Oh," she said, giving his crotch a squeeze as he turned the cart toward the driving range. "I can hardly wait."

"Neither can Hagar and Maxwell's men. We could put a show on for them."

"Sometimes you just take all the fun out of things," she said, pretending to pout, but not taking her hand from his crotch.

"I don't remember taking anything out of anything earlier this morning."

She just laughed and kept squeezing his crotch all the way to the driving range.

By the third hole Craig had shed his jacket.

By the fourth hole Bonnie was down to her tight yellow shorts and white blouse, getting a whistle of appreciation from the Senator that made her blush again. Craig loved the fact that he had a beautiful and smart wife. Sometimes he worried that she was going to leave him for someone better, but at times like today he just enjoyed her beauty and the fact that other men found her beautiful as well.

Actually, it turned out that riding together in the cart behind the Senator and Danny was more fun for Craig. He and Bonnie pointed out Maxwell and Hagar's men to each other, and between them could keep a pretty close eye on the Senator at all times. They made sure that one of them was always standing beside him on every green and tee box.

Plus every time Craig had a chance he touched her and she touched him. By the time this was all over he was going to be hot in more ways than just the temperature.

Craig felt as if they had passed a milestone when they reached the mountain-top tee for the sixteenth hole. Two more holes after this one and a quick lunch and the Senator would be on the way to the airport, out of his and Bonnie's vacation. He had come down here to play golf, spend time with Bonnie and get away from police work. Even though they had had fun so far, it would be nice to have at least one night to not think about life and death situations and protecting a United States Senator.

Just three more holes.

Craig grabbed a five iron and moved up to stand beside Bonnie and the Senator on the top-most tee box. This hole was so beautiful, he just wanted to stand and stare at the valley and mountains below them. The golf course architect had outdone himself when picking this tee box and putting the green down across the canyon. It would be a golf hole Craig would never forget. And one that would be impossible to describe to his friends back in Seattle.

Danny was up first and with his beautiful swing lofted a short iron into the air that floated seemingly forever before landing on the green pretty close to where his ball had been yesterday. Craig would be happy just to have his shot from yesterday again. It was his best of the tournament so far.

The Senator was up next and hit his first shot into the canyon that cut across in front of the green. Disgusted, he dropped another ball. "I'm going to get one over if I have to use every ball in my damned bag."

Bonnie laughed. "I've got an extra dozen you can use as well."

The Senator frowned at her joke. "Just watch this, young lady."

His next shot got into the air and for a moment Craig thought it just might make it over after all, but then it came down with a resounding smack right square in the middle of the wooden cart bridge that crossed the canyon near the right front of the green.

"Bulls-eye!" Bonnie yelled.

The ball bounced a good fifty feet into the air, and as they all watched open-mouthed, landed on the green and rolled up closer to the pin than Danny's ball.

Hagar and an FBI agent standing on the hillside behind the green applauded that shot, laughing and shaking their heads. Craig almost choked from the laughter, and Bonnie turned red trying to not laugh too hard.

The Senator, who was also laughing, seemed extraordinarily proud of himself. He picked up his tee and turned, a massive smile on his face. "I won't be needing those extra balls, thank you, young lady."

That broke them all up again. Craig shook the Senator's hand and Bonnie gave him a peck on the cheek before moving up to the tee. That shot was going to clearly be the highlight of all their rounds.

Bonnie proceeded to hit three into the canyon before she quit in disgust and with much teasing from the Senator about him lending her golf balls.

Craig managed to get his shot over, but barely, landing it in a pile of rocks far to the left of the green. Two shots in two days over the canyon. He was very proud of himself.

They were getting into the carts, still laughing and joking about the Senator's bridge shot, when suddenly Bonnie grabbed Craig's arm and whispered to him. "What if those two men weren't just passing through the cart shed last night?"

She pointed at the warning signs for the steep cart path they had to wind their way down. Who knew what would happen if the brakes failed on a cart on the way down this cliff face. Nothing good, that was for sure.

"Senator!" Bonnie shouted before the Senator could start off. He glanced back.

"Can we talk with you for a moment?" Craig asked.

The Senator was still smiling from his shot, but when he saw the frown on Craig's face, he nodded and climbed out of the cart to come back to them.

Maxwell, who had had been sitting in a cart just a few yards behind Bonnie and Craig, came up to see what they wanted as well.

Craig watched the Senator as he came back. Danny glanced around, clearly sweating, then turned back to stare over the valley below.

The little voice in Craig's head said Danny's reaction seemed odd. Very odd.

Maxwell reached Craig's side at the same time the Senator did.

"What's going on?" Maxwell asked.

Bonnie leaned over Craig in the cart to whisper to both of them. "I just realized that maybe those two men last night might have been in that cart shed for a reason. I remember hearing the sound of metal clanging on the concrete just a moment before we saw them."

"A tool?" Maxwell asked.

"Maybe," Craig said. "Did your men check the Senator's cart?"

"Just for explosives," Maxwell said, nodding and glancing at the hill in front of them.

"That's good to know," the Senator said, shaking his head at the thought of a bomb in his golf cart. "But I can tell you that the brakes have been working great on that cart. I'm sure it will make it down this."

"Let's let Danny take it just to make sure," Craig said. "Humor us, Senator."

"I agree," Maxwell said.

The Senator chuckled. "I suppose after that shot, I could use a little walk. At least it's downhill."

"I'll walk with you," Bonnie said, climbing out of the cart and moving around the cart to stand beside the Senator.

Maxwell nodded, turned, and moved up to the lead cart. "Danny, go ahead and take the cart to the green."

"But what about the Senator?" Danny asked, clearly sweating now.

Craig stared at the young pro and could clearly see the slight panic hidden just below the surface. Craig knew that look. He knew it from watching hundreds of criminals get caught in the act. Was it possible that Danny was in on the plan to hurt the Senator?

Maxwell glanced back at Craig. Clearly he had seen the same thing.

"The Senator feels like a walk," Maxwell said.

"That's a long ways, Senator," Danny said, clearly trying to get the Senator in the cart.

"Not with a beautiful woman it isn't," the Senator said, not seeming to notice Danny's discomfort.

"Go ahead," Maxwell said, patting the roof of Danny's cart as the young man reluctantly slid over into the driver's seat. "We'll meet you at the green."

Danny started off, going extra slow.

"Stay with the Senator," Craig whispered to Maxwell. "I'll follow Danny."

Maxwell nodded and quickly turned and spoke softly into a communications device he had in his watch. Craig saw one of the men on the far hill behind the green start down toward the green at once, with Hagar following.

Craig stayed a good twenty paces behind Danny as they went across the cliff face under the tee box and made the first switchback. Twice the kid looked over his shoulder at Craig with a very frightened look.

Craig only smiled.

Clearly the kid knew something, or was very, very afraid of driving a golf cart.

Craig was betting on the kid knowing something.

After the next switchback the cart path took a sharp drop as it crossed the steepest part of the cliff, then made another switchback seemingly out over space. It was the scariest corner on the hill and the most dangerous. There were warning signs to use brakes and watch speed, and there were bumps built into the path to remind any driver to keep the cart's speed down. On this cliff face, Craig couldn't imagine any golfer trying to go fast on purpose.

Or forgetting, for that matter.

Ahead of Craig there was a slight pop from the Senator's cart and Danny looked suddenly panicked.

Danny's cart seemed to shoot ahead, as if Danny had put his foot on the gas.

On a downhill slope most golf carts have inhibitors that slowed the cart if it got going too fast.

Danny's clearly did not, or was suddenly broken.

Danny was almost smashing his head on the roof as the cart banged over the warning bumps. He seemed frozen in panic, holding the wheel with both hands, his arms straight ahead.

The cart was heading into the switchback far, far too fast. It would never make it. Craig instantly knew what the plan had been.

With the Senator driving and on the cliff side, there would have been no chance for him to get out with Danny beside him. But there was no one blocking Danny.

"Jump!" Craig shouted.

Danny dove across the seat and out the passenger side at the last possible instant, just as the cart tipped toward the driver's side and went over the rock edge.

Somehow Danny managed to clear the cart, rolling once on the pavement and coming up hard against a rock with a sickening thud.

The cart, with the two sets of clubs rattling and banging, rolled over and over down the steep rock face, filling the valley with a smashing sound that echoed off the rock hills.

Clubs flew everywhere as the cart gathered speed end-over-end. The top of the cart ripped away like paper, spinning in the air. A couple of the heavy batteries under the seat flew away like large missiles.

Danny's massive golf bag came loose and did three end-over-end flips, scattering clubs and gear everywhere.

Fiberglass from the cart's side panel exploded in fragments as it smashed into a massive rock.

What was left of the cart finally did a quick flip and disappeared over the cliff face and into the deep canyon in front of the green. The sound of it smashing into the rocks and brush at the bottom was like nothing Craig had ever heard.

The echo of the sound took a long time to die off.

If the Senator had been in that cart, he could have easily been killed in the "accident."

Craig had his cart stopped and was bending over Danny as the young pro groaned and sat up. He was going to be bruised and scraped, but it didn't look like anything was broken.

"Don't move," Craig said.

Danny ignored him and tried to stand.

"I said don't move!"

"But I have—"

Craig flipped the kid over on his face on the cart path and pulled his arm behind it, leaning on the arm and Danny's back with one knee.

"You struggle and I break the arm," Craig said, using his weight to hold the younger man down. He wasn't going to take any chances with someone who could try to kill a Senator.

Danny spit out some gravel and blood. "Why are you doing this to me?"

"You know as well as I do," Craig said, pushing down even harder on the arm, making Danny jerk in pain and scrape the side of his face on the hot concrete path.

Craig glanced around. Both Hagar and the agent who had been behind the green were heading at a run up the cart path toward him. The agent was going to beat the local detective, but not by much. Maxwell was coming down the trail in a cart, going as fast as he dared. The Senator and Bonnie were out of sight up near the tee box.

"You're not going to be playing much golf where you're going," Craig said to Danny, pushing a little more on the arm and back with his knee. "Attempted murder of a United States Senator should get you about fifty years."

"But I didn't—"

Craig pressed down on Danny's arm just a little harder with his knee, cutting off the kid's excuse in a gasp of pain.

"The FBI guys are almost here," Craig said. "As a suggestion, I would recommend very highly you tell them everything. You might just get out in time to make the Seniors' tour if you do that. Maybe even earlier."

"You don't understand," Danny said, clearly on the edge of tears. "I had to. My wife. You don't understand."

Now the wife comment shocked Craig. He was about to ask another question when Maxwell slid the cart to a stop behind the one Craig had been in. At the same moment the agent from behind the green, clearly out of breath and sweating from the hard run in the heat, came around the switchback where the Senator's cart had gone over.

"Is he all right?" Maxwell asked as Craig got off the young pro and yanked Danny to his feet.

"For someone who's going to spend a large part of his youth in jail," Craig said, "I think so. Better read him his rights for attempted murder and whatever else you might want to add on. I think he might have a few things to say."

Maxwell nodded for the other agent to take Danny and do just that.

"Wait," Danny said. "I can get you who's behind this, but you have to save my wife."

Craig looked at Maxwell. Clearly Maxwell was just as puzzled as Craig was.

"Read him his rights," Maxwell said, "And then we'll talk."

Then into his communications watch Maxwell said, "Get the Senator down here and hidden in the canyon. Quick. And block entrances to this area from both sides. I want a medical evacuation helicopter here as quickly as possible, and a secure room ready in the hospital."

Craig was impressed. Maxwell was thinking clearly and quickly.

"The Senator went over in the cart, I assume," Craig said, smiling at Maxwell who was staring down the hill at the scattered clubs, parts of a cart roof, and Danny's almost empty bag.

"He had an accident, as far as the world is going to know tonight," Maxwell said.

At that point Hagar made it up the final stretch looking white and out of breath. Running up a steep hill in desert heat could hurt anyone. It clearly hadn't done Hagar any good.

Maxwell stepped over to Danny who was finished having his rights read to him by a still-out-of-breath and sweating agent. "So how can you help us?"

"I'm supposed to meet the man who kidnapped my wife tonight in my room at nine, if the Senator can't make the flight to Washington. And they will release her then."

"Release your wife?"

"They took her on Friday," Danny said, panic in his eyes. He had blood dripping down the side of his face and one leg looked like it had been scraped with sandpaper, but he wasn't seeming to notice. "They said they wanted to make sure I would help. If I didn't, or told the police, they were going to kill her and me."

Maxwell nodded. "So why did you go ahead and wreck the cart without the Senator in it?"

"I didn't do that," Danny said. "The brakes failed like they were supposed to. I was just insurance, to make sure that if the brakes didn't fail, I made the cart go over the edge with the Senator in it. But don't you see, I had to, to save my wife."

Craig shook his head. "You and your wife would have never lived to see your home again."

Danny looked even paler than he had a moment before.

Maxwell nodded. "People who would do this can't leave witnesses."

Maxwell glanced back up the cart path. Then to the agent Maxwell pointed at the spot where the cart path became very steep. "Sweep that hillside for a buried transmitter. I bet we'll find a matching one inside the braking system of the cart."

Craig glanced down the cliff face. "If there's anything left of the cart."

Maxwell glanced down the hill. "There'll be enough. Let's just hope they were stupid enough to leave us some prints as well."

"Oh, my," the Senator said as he and Bonnie and another agent came down the path. "Danny, are you all right?"

"I'm so sorry, Senator," Danny said. Then he dropped to the path and broke into sobs.

"Danny?" the Senator said, clearly shocked as he stared at the young pro, then at Craig and Maxwell.

Craig stepped toward Bonnie and the Senator. Bonnie gave him a quick hug.

"It seems Danny was blackmailed into helping them," Craig said. "And I'm afraid, Senator, that you're not going to get a chance to make that birdie putt."

The Senator glanced down over the edge of the cart path at the scattered clubs and parts of a cart on the steep, rocky cliff, clearly understanding how close he had just come to being hurt or killed. "I doubt my putter survived that crash anyway."

"Senator," Maxwell said, "we need you down near the canyon so we can airlift you out. Just in case the wrong people end up watching."

"I'm going to the hospital, huh?" the Senator asked, clearly understanding the plan.

"Actually, yes," Maxwell said. "And then directly to the airport where you'll catch a flight to Washington under complete secrecy."

"Sounds like a plan," he said to Maxwell. "Good luck catching whoever is behind this."

"We'll have a report to you tomorrow," Maxwell said. "We only have to keep the charade up for the night."

The Senator nodded, then turned to Bonnie and Craig. "I don't know even where to start thanking you."

He shook Craig's hand firmly, then Bonnie gave him a kiss.

"It's been our pleasure, Senator," Bonnie said. "Thirty-three of the most enjoyable holes of golf I have ever played."

The Senator laughed and stepped back and looked at Bonnie's tight shorts and white blouse. "Young lady, trust me, it has been my pleasure as well."

With a laugh at Bonnie's blushing red face, the Senator winked at Craig and turned and headed down the cart path.

All Craig could do was chuckle at his beautiful wife.

Twelve minutes later the Senator was airlifted out on a stretcher, headed for the hospital and his home in Washington.

CHAPTER FOURTEEN

Sunday, April 9th
2:36 p.m.

BONNIE SAT ON the bed with Craig in a room on the hotel's top floor and watched as the last of Danny's scrapes were treated.

Clearly Maxwell and the other FBI agents had been using this room as a base. It was bigger than her and Craig's room, yet considerably smaller than the Senator's massive suite. From the looks of the table and kitchen area, a number of agents had been going and coming from here twenty-fours hours a day. Right now Maxwell and three agents were here, as well as Hagar and Danny. The agent working on Danny's cuts and scrapes clearly had a good knowledge of first aid.

After the Senator was airlifted away, they had decided that to get Danny back into the hotel without arousing suspicion, she and Craig would walk him in. It would be logical that if he wasn't under suspicion for any crime, that he would be with his playing companions.

As Danny was being treated, he told what had happened to him and his wife over the last week. To Bonnie the story he told had a ring of truth through it. But on top of that, she wanted to believe him. Craig was clearly not so sure.

It seemed that on Friday morning, while Danny was at his golf course for a few hours, Danny's wife, Steph, was taken from their apartment in Sedona. Danny guessed that there had been three, but by the time he got home only one was waiting for him. Danny had seen the man who wasn't masked a few times this weekend around the hotel, and the guy had come to Danny's room last night.

Danny said he had told the man that he wouldn't cooperate unless he could have proof his wife was alive every day. Danny looked up at Maxwell. "They threatened to kill her, but I held to my demand."

Maxwell nodded. "Go on. What did they do then?"

"They let me talk to her for a few seconds Friday night late, and again last night," he said, barely holding it together.

Craig glanced at Maxwell. Bonnie knew exactly what Craig was thinking. If there were phone calls, there could be traces on those calls. Maxwell nodded, clearly thinking along the same lines.

He turned to one of three agents standing nearby. "Get Danny's room and home phone records and get those calls traced."

"They weren't on my room phone," Danny said. "The guy always handed me a cell phone and told me to punch redial."

"Damn," Maxwell said.

"How about the face of the phone?" Bonnie asked. "Could you see the number?"

Danny shook his head. "The guy had it taped over."

"Smart," Hagar said.

Bonnie had to agree.

"It was so hard," Danny said, "not calling the police."

"You should have, you know," Maxwell said.

"I do now," Danny said softly. "But I was so afraid they were going to kill her."

Bonnie had no doubt not calling the police was going to be one decision Danny would regret for a long time. But now wasn't the time to dwell on that.

"What did they say was going to happen?" Craig asked.

"That an accident was going to hurt the Senator during the golf tournament today, and I was to make sure the accident happened no matter what.

"Did they say what kind of accident?" Maxwell asked.

"Just a cart accident on a steep hill," Danny said. "When I saw the 16th hole yesterday I knew that was where it would happen. They said if the Senator was too injured to get on the plane, my wife would be released tonight. If not, I would never see her again. And they would make sure I never saw anyone again."

"Get on the plane?" Hagar asked, stepping closer to Danny. "You sure he used those exact words?"

Bonnie had been just about to ask that same question, but Hagar beat her to it. That detail had to be an important part of finding who was behind this.

Danny nodded at Hagar. "That's what he said."

"The vote tomorrow against Charles Robins' companies?" Craig asked Maxwell.

"Sure seems that way," Maxwell said. "We've had the Robins' estate under surveillance since the accident."

There was a silence in the room.

"Okay, what time are you to meet your contact?" Maxwell asked.

"Six, in my room," Danny said.

"It's four now," Hagar said, glancing at his watch.

"Okay, we need to get you down there and set up," Maxwell said. "We want to catch your contact to find out where they are keeping your wife. And who they are working for."

"That's going to be a problem," Bonnie said. "What happens if someone is watching? Danny can't go into this meeting alone, but going into his room with one of your agents might stop the entire thing."

"I agree," Hagar said. "These people were sophisticated enough to blow the brakes on a golf cart at the right point, it would be easy for them to be watching Danny's room."

"Maybe even have it bugged, just in case," Craig said.

Bonnie couldn't agree more.

"My room's been bugged?" Danny asked, clearly trying to keep up with all this.

"In all likelihood that's exactly right," Maxwell said.

"How about Craig and I go to Danny's room with him," Bonnie said, "stage a leaving, and hide out in the room until Danny's contact shows up."

Maxwell nodded. "Might work. We can have you all wired and we can be staged in rooms in both directions down the hall to block any retreat."

"If we're not going to take a chance of being seen," Craig said, "I don't see any other choice."

Neither did she.

Just under one hour later she and Craig were walking with Danny from the elevator to his room, not really talking. Bonnie could feel the heaviness of the police-issue pistol against the small of her back, its metal cool in the air-conditioned hotel. It was the only place on her they could find to hide it safely. Craig had his tucked in the side of his belt and his golf shirt pulled out to cover it.

Danny had memorized a few lines, and understood completely that he wasn't to talk to Craig and Bonnie after they said good-bye just inside his room.

She and Craig were going to station themselves inside Danny's bedroom in the small suite. The moment Danny's contact was let into the suite, Hagar and Maxwell and their people would be outside the door, ready to come through within ten seconds.

A very long ten seconds, as far as Bonnie was concerned. While Danny was in the bathroom getting ready to go, Maxwell had told Bonnie and Craig and Hagar that he suspected that the contact wasn't there for information about the Senator, but to kill Danny.

Maxwell figured they were going to have to move fast.

The plan was that Danny was to let the man into the room, and close the door, giving Maxwell and Hagar enough time to get into position before coming through. When Bonnie and Craig heard Maxwell break in, they were to come in from the bedroom. At that moment Danny was to drop to the floor and stay there.

It was a sound plan, but Bonnie had a fear it wasn't going to work like they hoped. She didn't know why she felt that way. More than likely just jitters.

It had been a long time, since she had been involved in something like this. And then only once in her second year on the force. This was much more of what Craig did in his job as a detective. She very seldom had to stage raids on homes of domestically abused children. Usually she and her people just went in with a warrant and took the children out. At times it got ugly, but she always had plenty of help.

They reached Danny's room without seeing anyone else in the hallway.

She knew that Hagar and Maxwell and their people had already taken their positions one-at-a-time in rooms along the hall. And more than likely Hagar and Maxwell had just watched the three of them walk by.

Craig and Bonnie were also wired for sound, but Danny wasn't, just in case the first thing the contact did was pat him down.

Danny fumbled with the key card, then managed to get the door open. They all stepped inside and the door closed. The first thing Danny did was move to the windows and draw the curtains in both the living area and the bedroom.

Then as Danny stood with Bonnie near the door, looking scared, Craig, gun drawn, silently and quickly checked out the rooms of the small suite to make sure no one else was in there. When he came out of the bedroom and nodded, Bonnie went into her script. If someone was listening, it needed to be clear to them what was happening.

"Are you sure you're going to be all right?" she asked.

"I think so," Danny said. "Just shaken up."

Bonnie nodded to him that he was doing fine. He looked like he might be sick at any moment.

"Understandable," Craig said. "But it was an accident. Remember that."

"Sure," Danny said, his voice shaking. "Thanks."

"You going to be all right?" Bonnie asked. "You want us to stay with you for a little bit?"

"No, thanks," Danny said, staying with the script they had worked out. "I think I just need to rest."

"All right," Craig said. "We'll meet you for dinner at seven in the restaurant."

"Sounds good," Danny said.

Bonnie opened the door, then let it close a moment later with a loud thump. Her own heart seemed to be pounding even harder and she was sure Maxwell and his people could hear every beat through the microphone taped inside her blouse.

Craig held his finger to his lips in the motion for all of them to be very silent. Then he moved over and turned on the television, putting it on one of the movie channels at a moderate volume.

He pointed to the couch for Danny to sit, then motioned for Bonnie to come with him into the bedroom.

Craig eased the door almost closed behind them, leaving just enough of a crack in the door that he could see Danny sitting like a statue on the couch.

Bonnie glanced around at Danny's clothes from yesterday tossed on the chair, and an unopened Star Trek paperback book on the dresser. Then she glanced at Craig.

He gave her a quick thumbs-up sign.

Now all they had to do was wait.

Silently.

Chapter Fifteen

Sunday, April 9th
5:31 p.m.

CHARLES ROBINS STARED at the ringing phone for a few moments, then decided he might as well answer it. Last night he hadn't slept much, and all morning he felt as if he was walking in a haze. He could never remember feeling like this before.

The phone that was ringing was a private number known only to a few people. The man working for him today was not one of them, but Charles had no doubt the man knew it.

Charles moved across his lavishly furnished study to the cell phone sitting on the corner of his oak desk. He hadn't asked the man for an update, but somehow he expected one since the extra demand for money.

How else was he to know when to pay?

He picked up the phone on the fourth ring and said, "Yes."

The man's distinctive voice filled Charles's mind as if the volume on his phone was turned up high.

"Oh, pardon the interruption," the man said, his voice as level and controlled as always. "I was trying to call the hospital."

The line went dead and Charles put the phone down. He didn't know how he felt. Clearly Senator Knight was in the hospital, the man's mission accomplished as planned. But he wouldn't let just one phone call be his confirmation.

Charles moved over to a wall cabinet and opened it so his large television was exposed. He quickly turned it on and flipped to a local Phoenix news channel. They were covering the Senator's tragic accident, as he would have expected they would. It seemed the Senator's cart had gone out of control on a steep path and rolled down a rocky slope. The Senator had been airlifted to the hospital where his condition was considered critical.

Charles flipped off the television and moved back to his desk. He was feeling even more numb than he had earlier, but he was sure a good night's sleep would solve that problem. And now that his companies were out of immediate danger from the good Senator, he just might get some sleep.

He dropped down into his chair and clicked on his computer screen. He had the money set up to transfer to the man's account after it was confirmed about the Senator. But it wasn't as much as the man had demanded. In fact, it was nowhere near as much.

Charles glanced at the total, then laughed. "You think you can blackmail me, do you?" With a click the funds were transferred to the man's account. "I can change the rules just as easily as you can," Charles said to the man, as if he could hear, "and there isn't a damn thing you can do about it. Not with the security I've got around here. You work for me, remember?"

With a laugh Charles shut down his computer and stood. "A good brandy and a steak for dinner is just what the doctor ordered."

Charles laughed again, starting to feel a lot better. "Probably not the Senator's doctor."

CHAPTER SIXTEEN

Sunday, April 9th
5:47 p.m.

TO CRAIG THE first fifteen minutes of waiting seemed to drag on and on as they stood just inside Danny's bedroom door.

Bonnie paced silently while he leaned against the door frame. Every thirty seconds or so he peeked through the slightly open door to make sure Danny was still sitting on the couch. The young golf pro was, watching television and doing his best to remain still, mostly without success.

But his orders from Maxwell were to stay on the couch, without moving around, until the man showed up, and that was exactly what Danny was doing.

Craig couldn't blame the kid for squirming and worrying. He was in a situation different from anything he had ever seen outside a movie. And his wife had been taken hostage all because of someone's desire to get to a United States Senator. How completely unfair was that?

If that was what had really happened.

At first Craig hadn't believed the kid, but over the last hour he had started to. Craig's biggest worry now was that Danny's wife was already dead. There was no doubt that the Senator would be injured or dead and Danny might be facing a death sentence shortly if he and Bonnie hadn't accidentally overheard that conversation the first night. But finding Danny's wife was another matter.

Right now Maxwell and his people were scrambling to triangulate cell calls and track down any lead that might give them a clue to Steph Baines's location.

Bonnie found a hotel note pad on the nightstand beside the phone and scribbled a quick note, holding it up to him to see.

This waiting is driving me nuts!

Craig smiled at her and nodded his agreement. They still had almost thirty minutes before the man Danny was supposed to meet was even scheduled to show.

Craig took the pen and pad and wrote a note back to her.

Me too. Wish we had turned the television on in here as well.

She read his note and nodded. Then took the pad and wrote:
That would have helped.

They wrote a few notes back and forth for the next ten minutes until suddenly there was a knock on the hall door into Danny's room.

Craig checked on Danny through the crack in the open door. The young pro was staring his way, a very frightened look on his face.

Craig silently opened the bedroom door enough for Danny to see him and motioned for Danny to go ahead and let his contact into the suite.

Danny took a deep breath and went for the door as Craig eased the bedroom door closed and pulled his gun, quickly checking it to make sure it was loaded and ready to fire.

Bonnie had her gun in her hand as well. Her face was flushed and she was fighting to control her breathing. That knock must have really startled her.

It startled him, that was for sure, even though that was what they had been waiting for.

He motioned for her to take a position on the far side of the dresser behind where the door would open.

Craig then moved over against the wall by the closet so he would have a clear angle at the doorway. If the guy checked in here before Maxwell and Hagar came in, Craig planned on greeting the guy with a loaded gun, and he wanted Bonnie flanking the man, but not in his line of fire.

Also he and Bonnie had worked out that if they had to go through the door, he would go first and to his left, she second and to the right. These starting positions would make it easier for that to happen.

Bonnie got into position and nodded she was ready.

"Yeah," Danny said as he opened the doorway into the hall.

A very long pause.

Craig glanced at Bonnie and motioned that she should take a deep breath. She did, silently, then mouthed to him to be careful.

"I see our Senator had himself a little accident, as planned," a man's voice said as the door to the hall closed.

Craig glanced at Bonnie, whose eyes were wide. She recognized the voice as well as he did. It was one of the guys they had overheard on Friday night.

"My wife?" Danny asked. "Is she all right?"

"Ahh, sure thing, kid," the man said. "Right as rain. You and her can be doing the humpy-bumpy tonight."

"So when can I talk to her?" Danny demanded.

Craig glanced at his watch. Thirteen seconds had gone by. Maxwell and Hagar should be coming through the door at any instant.

"I'm goin' to take you to a place where you can talk to her," the man said.

Craig knew that the place the man wanted to take Danny to was where Danny would be killed.

"No!" Danny said. "I want to talk to her now!"

Craig glanced at Bonnie, whose eyes were round. That wasn't in Danny's script.

"Sure, kid," the man said. "No skin off my nose."

Craig could hear the beeping of a cell phone as the man dialed a number. If he was actually dialing the location of Danny's wife, Craig hoped Maxwell and the others were listening and would give the call time to happen. That way they had something to triangulate to find the location.

"Put the kid's wife on the phone again," the man said.

Then Danny said, "Steph? Are you all right?"

There was a pause.

"I love you," Danny said.

"That's enough, kid," the man said. "You'll see her soon enough."

There was a clear sound of the cell phone cover being snapped shut. "Now, let's go."

At that instant the door from the hall burst open and Maxwell's voice shouted "FBI!"

Craig took one step toward the bedroom door and yanked it open, moving left, his gun aimed at the man standing near the television. The guy looked to be no more than thirty and couldn't have been taller than five-foot-five.

Danny dove away from the man for the couch, rolling over a coffee table as he went.

The man drew a revolver from under his coat jacket, spinning at Maxwell coming through the hallway door.

"Don't!" Craig shouted.

"Drop the gun!" Maxwell shouted.

The guy didn't listen.

It was a very stupid thing not to do.

The guy had his gun out and was turning on Maxwell when both Craig and Maxwell fired.

The two shots slammed the room in sound.

Craig was aiming at the man's shoulder and arm. From fifteen feet, he knew he didn't miss.

Maxwell was even closer and clearly didn't miss either.

The man spun around like someone had put a boogie-board under his feet and yanked on him. His gun banged against the wall from the force of the impacts and ended up near the small bar.

The man did a complete three hundred and sixty degree turn and smashed to the floor, face up, staring at the ceiling, his legs twisted under him.

The noise inside the small room was deafening from the two shots and the air stank of gunpowder. Craig had had to fire his gun in a few enclosed areas before, and the intensity of the explosion and smell always caught him by surprise.

Both Craig and Maxwell were over the man before he even stopped falling. Craig could see that the guy had been hit twice. Once in the right shoulder, which was Craig's shot, and once in the stomach, which had to be Maxwell's. The guy clearly wasn't going anywhere. He was going to be lucky to live.

Now the copperish odor of blood filled the air, mixing with the gunpowder smell as blood stained the carpet black below the guy.

Maxwell bent down over the man, whose eyes were fluttering like he had sand in them.

Craig glanced around at Bonnie, who was standing over Danny, her hand on his shoulder as he sobbed into the couch. Two other agents and Hagar were also in the room.

"Ambulance," Craig said and Hagar grabbed the phone off the stand beside him.

"And get the number of that last call and its location," Maxwell said, picking the cell phone out of the man's front pocket and tossing it to one of the agents. "Stat!"

The agent with the phone grabbed it out of the air, jumped toward the door, and disappeared into the hall.

"Who hired you?" Maxwell asked, turning back to the man on the floor.

The guy stopped blinking long enough to look at Maxwell, then at Craig.

Craig knew the look. It was an awareness of death coming, as if suddenly a person knew death now and accepted it all in one instant. Craig had seen it on every death he had witnessed. The guy had the look now.

"Come on," Maxwell said, urgency in his voice. "Who hired you?"

The guy looked like he wanted to say something.

The silence as they tried to listen for what the man would say seemed extra intense in the room after the sound of shots.

But there was going to be nothing but silence.

All that came out of the guy's mouth were a few bloody bubbles before he died.

Chapter Seventeen

Sunday, April 9th
7:01 p.m.

BONNIE HAD BEEN a cop long enough to see her share of death. And every time she hoped she would never have to see more.

This time was no different.

Just easier.

The deaths of children and teenagers were the ones that bothered her the most, but every death seemed to carve a small chunk out of her soul, leaving her feeling just a little more empty and a little more jaded toward life and people.

Having the guy die in the fight in the hotel room was startling, and disturbing, but for some reason she didn't find herself that upset about it. He had tried to kill Senator Knight, had kidnapped Danny's wife, and was more than likely going to kill Danny and his wife if they had given him time.

Having him die wasn't a great loss to the world, the way she figured it. She knew that was cold, but sometimes being a cop made you cold when it came to scum.

Craig clearly felt the same way. Craig seemed more upset that he was going to have to do massive paperwork and attend post-shooting hearings after all this was over. Hagar had promised him he would help speed the process. And if he did have to come back for a hearing, just think of the golf he could play. That comment had cheered Craig up some.

Right now she and Craig and the rest were much more worried about getting Danny's wife recovered safely. The cell phone they had gotten off the dead guy was stolen, and the number called had been to another stolen cell phone.

No surprise there.

Maxwell and his team had managed to get the area the cell call went into narrowed down to a ten-block radius in a Phoenix suburb. But the only way to pinpoint the call exactly to one location was to call the number again.

And somehow keep the line open long enough to get a fix on the location.

With the help of the Scottsdale police, the Phoenix police, and other agencies nearby, they had quietly blocked off the entire ten-block area and were standing ready to swarm in on the location as soon as they had it pinpointed. There was going to be no talking with whoever was holding Danny's wife. They were going to swarm in and take her back without warning.

Danny seemed ready as well to help in getting his wife to safety. They had all gone back up to the FBI's room on the top floor of the hotel, leaving Danny's room for the crime scene people and FBI to go over. Maxwell had figured if Danny made the phone call, there might be more of a chance of it staying connected long enough to get an exact location pinpointed.

Bonnie agreed and was standing beside Danny, with Craig on the other side, when Maxwell said, "Ready."

Danny nodded and pressed redial on the dead man's cell phone. Then he carefully put it to his ear as if he was afraid it might explode on him.

Bonnie forced herself to let out the breath she was holding and put her hand gently on Danny's shoulder to let him know they were there for him.

After a short moment Danny said, "The guy said I could talk to my wife again."

A slight pause.

Danny looked panicked.

"He's right here," Danny said. "Just put my wife on."

Behind Danny, Maxwell signaled thumbs up.

They had the location and were closing in. But he wanted Danny to keep talking if he could. It would be better for those moving in to keep the guy on the line and busy somehow.

"All right, all right," Danny said. "You can talk to him. Then let me talk to my wife again will ya?"

Bonnie was impressed at the young pro. He had played it perfectly.

Danny glanced at Bonnie with the phone held out in front of him. He had the questioning look of what was he supposed to do now? He had gone through all his lines they had worked on and he clearly wasn't capable of making something up in his state of mind.

Craig motioned for Danny to talk into the phone again, but Bonnie could tell Danny was clearly about to lose it. This was all far, far beyond his depth.

Bonnie shook her head at her husband, signaling him to not push the young pro any more.

Craig glanced at Maxwell, then took the phone. He smiled at her and gave her his nothing-to-lose-shrug.

She agreed. They had pinpointed the location and at this point they had nothing to lose and everything to gain by keeping whoever was on the other end of the line busy for just a few more seconds.

"Let him talk to his wife, fer cryin' out loud," Craig said.

Bonnie was impressed. Craig's voice sounded like a passable imitation of the dead-man's voice. Sometimes her husband's hidden skills were just amazing.

"Yeah, yeah, I know," Craig said after a short moment, "but the kid wouldn't budge without another call."

Suddenly Craig held the phone away from his ear. Bonnie could hear the sounds of gunfire coming from the phone. One shot, another two quick ones, then nothing.

Craig carefully put the cell phone back up to his ear and listened for a moment, then shook his head that there was nothing on the other end.

They all looked at Maxwell.

"Is Steph all right?" Danny asked Maxwell.

He said nothing.

Bonnie could feel her stomach clamping down hard as she waited. Beside her Danny seemed as if he might just faint from the fear and worry and waiting.

Maxwell was listening to reports from his people on headphones. Suddenly he broke into a big smile at Danny. "They have her."

"She's all right?" Danny asked, his voice weak and shaking.

"She's all right," Maxwell said, smiling the broadest grin Bonnie could have imagined the man smiling. "They're taking her to the hospital. You can meet her there."

At that Danny just slumped into a chair and broke down and started crying.

For a moment the hardened cops and agents in the room looked at the young golf pro with stunned looks.

Then Bonnie sat down beside him and put her arm on his shoulder for comfort. He deserved a good cry.

Around her a lot of men were smiling, including her husband. It looked like this was over for the moment.

And for a change, real life had a happy ending, even if the guy was crying.

CHAPTER EIGHTEEN

Sunday, April 9th
8:37 p.m.

THE MAN CHARLES Robins called Bill signaled for the limo driver to stop in a parking lot as he checked the account balance on his laptop computer screen one more time just to make sure.

It came up the same.

Charles Robins had shorted him exactly a half million dollars on the final payment.

"Stupid idiot," the man said.

He snapped the computer closed and put it back in his case.

Then as he was looking out the window of the limo, he started to laugh. "Stupid men always make stupid mistakes."

He had always known that Charles Robins was a stupid man, so this final act of greed was no surprise. It was mostly luck and underhanded dealings that had allowed Robins to build his house-of-cards fortune. The man had known that before he went to work for Robins. For years he had waited for this exact moment, the exact right opportunity to strike at Robins, take as much of Robins's money as he could, and move on.

He had gotten a half million out of the idiot. And now Robins had made the fatal mistake of not paying the rest. It was time to show Robins that there were some things not even an idiot could buy his way out of.

The man signaled for the driver to start up again, then reached into a briefcase and pulled out a cell phone. It was one of ten stolen for this operation that he hadn't used yet.

He punched in the number for the man he called Benny. The guy was all New York and proud of it. Benny didn't know the man's real name and he didn't know Benny's. They simply helped each other out when help was needed.

The phone rang three times too many without being picked up.

The man instantly clicked off his phone and punched the button for the window beside him to roll down. He used a handkerchief to carefully wipe off his fingerprints from the phone and the keypad. There was a stretch of empty desert and litter a few hundred feet ahead. As the limo went past he tossed the phone into the litter beside the road.

He put the window up and then keyed in the intercom to the driver of the limo. "Turn right at the next corner and then right again at the next and head back into town."

"Understood, sir," the driver said.

He sat back and thought. Was it possible that Benny had just put the phone down? By this time of night he should have already been at the house with Danny the golf pro. And both Danny and his young wife should be dead, if Benny followed orders. He was hoping to make use of the two bodies.

Was it possible that Benny was busy with that chore?

The man nodded and pulled out another cell phone. He punched in another number, this one for the phone of Benny's assistant who had been guarding the young wife.

The phone rang two too many rings before a voice answered. "Yeah."

The voice sounded like Benny's voice, but it wasn't Benny.

He clicked the cell phone closed, quickly wiped it clean of his fingerprints, and tossed it out the window. It bounced under a parked car.

"Driver, take a left at the next corner and go until you reach the freeway. Then head for Tucson."

"Yes, sir," the driver said.

It was clear that Benny and one of his men were either dead or captured by the FBI. It made sense that they would get the young pro to break the moment the Senator had his accident. And from there the trail was easy to Benny and his helper. He was going to miss Benny, that was for sure. A good worker.

But he wasn't going to miss the money he now didn't have to pay Benny. That was an extra bonus.

But what to do about Charles Robins?

The man sat back in the comfort of the limo and sipped a brandy, thinking. He wasn't halfway to Tucson before he came up with a great plan.

CHAPTER NINETEEN

Sunday, April 9th
11:21 p.m.

CRAIG PUSHED AWAY his mostly empty plate and sipped on the Diet Coke. They had been lucky to find a place with food this good so late on a Sunday night. It looked more like a diner stuffed inside an old freight warehouse, but Hagar had sworn by the place and he had been right. Great service, great food, and background music low enough to talk over.

What more could they have asked for?

At the moment Hagar was finishing a large plate of some sort of Mexican food Craig didn't recognize.

Maxwell had already pushed away the last of his barbecue chicken.

Bonnie was trying to polish off the last few pieces of her steak.

Around them there were still people coming in and being seated. Clearly the locals knew this place well. Craig couldn't imagine how busy it was during peak hours if there were this many people here on a late Sunday night.

For all of them it had been one very long day, topped with the scene in the hospital with Danny and Steph getting back together. Just the memory of that made Craig smile. The quiet, sullen young golf pro that they had played golf with all weekend suddenly had become happy, full of life, with a light in his eyes as he and his wife hugged and cried together.

Craig couldn't even imagine playing golf while Bonnie was being held hostage. But Danny had done what he thought he had to do. And somehow had managed. He was one strong kid.

From what Maxwell had said, because of Danny's help getting to some of the men behind the attempt on the Senator's life, and the situation of his wife being kidnapped, no charges against Danny would be brought. He and Steph were just victims of the larger plan.

At the hospital Craig had apologized to Danny for treating him so roughly on the cart path after the accident.

Danny said it was all right. For not calling the police at once he deserved much more than that. Then he had added that he never wanted to ever be on the receiving end of being arrested again by an angry cop. Once was enough.

Initially Craig and Bonnie had been scheduled to fly out early in the morning and be back to work on Tuesday from this so-called vacation. But since Craig had been involved in the shooting of one of the suspects, there were going to be hearings to attend and paperwork to fill out.

Bonnie had called the airline and pushed their flight back to Tuesday. Then she had told their bosses in Seattle what had happened. So with an extra day or so, maybe, just maybe, they could end up having a little time alone.

"So what happens next?" Bonnie asked Maxwell as she gave up and pushed her plate away from her with a few bites of steak still left.

Maxwell shrugged. "Steph Baines said there were three men who kidnapped her. Two are now dead, so we still got one out there somewhere."

"The guy who made the phone calls to the cell phones?" Craig asked.

Craig's attempt to imitate one of the dead men on the second call had failed instantly. Clearly the man making the calls was smart and was being very careful. Both calls had been made from different stolen cell phones, and both phones had been quickly found, obviously tossed out of a moving car.

"More than likely he's the third," Maxwell said, nodding as he sipped a cup of coffee. "And he's now a good distance out of the area."

"But he wasn't the money man," Hagar said.

"I doubt it," Maxwell said. "We're pretty sure that is Robins. He's the only one with motive to hurt the Senator. But proving it without the third man in custody is going to be damned hard."

"Money trail?" Bonnie asked.

"Maybe," Maxwell said. "If we can get the warrants, and if he was just plain stupid."

Craig could only nod his agreement. He doubted Robins was that stupid.

"Is the Senator safely in Washington?" Bonnie asked, her voice low so only the four of them could hear the question.

"Safe and ready for a press conference right before he goes in for the vote tomorrow morning," Maxwell said, smiling. "All his close family and friends have been informed of the ruse so they won't worry."

"Even without being caught it seems that Robins is going to get his just desserts," Craig said. "I'd love to see his face as he watches that press conference."

All of them laughed and agreed.

Craig glanced at Hagar. "When are you going to want me in the station tomorrow morning?"

Hagar looked at his watch. "How about at the crack of noon?"

"Perfect," Craig said, feeling relieved that Hagar hadn't said eight. "Just over twelve hours of vacation."

"A good night's sleep," Bonnie said, sighing. "Won't that be a change for this trip?"

"Let me know what it feels like," Maxwell said.

"Yeah, me too," Hagar agreed.

Thirty minutes later Hagar dropped them off in front of the hotel and twenty minutes after that they were in their swimming suits and sitting in the bubbling water of the hotel's massive hot tub.

The tub was located in a corner of the swimming pool area. It was surrounded by boulders and made to look more like a natural hot springs than a hotel hot tub. Craig had to admit that was a nice touch. And the best part was that when sitting down in the tub, the boulders blocked the view of the pool and the hotel, leaving nothing but the rocky mountainside above the hotel and the night stars. It made for a wonderful relaxing hot dip in what felt like a mountain pool.

They were alone in the hot tub since it was almost one in the morning, but another couple was sitting on the far side of the pool, holding hands and talking while their feet dangled in the water.

"Perfect temperature," Bonnie said, letting her body float with the bubbles beside him. "A great meal and a hot soak. I think I needed this."

"I couldn't agree more," he said, leaning back and letting the warm water soothe his nerves. "Only one thing I need more than this and sleep."

She laughed. "And just what might that be?"

Without looking at her he said, "You have to ask?"

Her hand moved over and rested on his crotch. "What do you have in mind?"

"Maybe an hour of sex in that big bed upstairs," he said, "then eight hours of sleep, then another hour of sex tomorrow morning."

"Before or after breakfast?" she asked.

"On second thought," he said, "maybe both."

"Oh, feeling young, are we?"

"What are vacations for?"

She laughed as her hand moved slowly on him for a moment and he hardened under her touch.

Then she said, "That's a perfect plan if you add in just one thing."

"Trust me," he said, "the thing you're playing with is part of the plan."

She laughed again, but didn't stop moving her hand. "No, I just wanted to stay in the hot tub for a few more minutes. Let some of the tension drain away."

"Before we go back to the room and create more tension?" he asked.

"Exactly," she said.

Maybe, just maybe, they might be able to salvage this vacation after all.

CHAPTER TWENTY

Monday, April 10th
1:06 a.m.

CHARLES ROBINS SAT back in his chair and smiled as Grant reported the security measures being taken around the estate.

Charles figured that if he was going to have a problem with the man he called Bill because of the short payment, it was going to be tonight.

Or maybe tomorrow night.

So he had called in every member of his security team, under the leadership of Grant, an ex-Marine who knew more about defense and killing than Charles ever wanted to know.

He had told Grant who he needed kept out and Grant had said it would be no problem.

His people would keep everyone out.

Charles was just fine with that.

Grant had just finished explaining the basic defenses of the estate. He had two dozen men, all with state-of-the-art weapons patrolling both the grounds and the house. Three men watched the security monitors at all times, taking shifts. Automatic alarms had been set on every inch of the grounds' parameter. Grant was convinced that nothing was coming in that they didn't know about.

"Only one problem I see, Mr. Robins," Grant said.

"What's that?" Robins asked. The last thing he needed tonight was problems. So far everything had gone perfectly. Senator Knight wouldn't be voting later in the day and that was just about as perfect as it got.

"An FBI surveillance van is parked across the street from the main gate," Grant said without moving his hands from the parade rest position he had been standing in for five minutes, "and they have three other men stationed around the parameter of the estate in observation locations."

"FBI?" Robins asked, his stomach suddenly twisting in fear. "Are you sure?"

"Yes, sir," Grant said, "I'm sure. You pay me to be sure."

"Any idea why they are out there?" Robins asked.

"No, sir."

"Are they making any move to come in?" Robins asked.

Grant shook his head. "No, sir. They are strictly in surveillance mode."

Robins nodded. "So anyone coming in here would have to get past them as well as your people."

"No one will get past my people," Grant said. "But the FBI, in the configuration they are working out of, would make no move to stop anyone. The fight would be ours, sir."

Robins nodded. "Thank you, Grant. I will talk to you in the early morning."

"Have a good evening, sir," Grant said. He spun and moved briskly out of the study, the heels of his boots making no sound on the hardwood floor.

FBI? What were they doing out there?

He felt himself panic and he forced himself to take a few deep breaths, his palms flat on the hard wood of his desk top.

Clearly someone had put the vote tomorrow, and the implications to his companies' future, together with the Senator's accident. And since the FBI had failed in keeping the Senator from having his little spill down the hill, it would make sense they would cover all bases.

He forced himself to take more deep breaths and relax and think.

If anyone could prove anything, or even had a shred of evidence besides speculation, the FBI would have come in and taken him. So the fact that they were just in observation mode was good news as well.

That thought released his fear.

Of course. They had nothing on him but motive. And motive wasn't enough to move against someone like him, even if they did prove it wasn't an accident.

Charles stood and moved over to his bar and poured himself a small glass of his finest scotch. It was almost time to get some sleep. The legislation that would have killed his companies would not be passed. And by the time it could come up again, he would have enough votes controlled to stop it completely.

He had won.

He should learn to relax a little and savor the victories.

He downed the Scotch and moved toward the back entrance of his study that led up to his bedroom.

A few hours sleep was exactly what he needed.

CHAPTER TWENTY-ONE

Monday, April 10th
1:37 a.m.

BONNIE KNEW THAT even with Craig's plans of sex tonight and to-morrow morning—which she liked the sound of a lot—they were going to be lucky to stay awake long enough to make it happen. The last two days had been very stressful to both of them, and after the dip in the soothing warm water of the hot tub, Craig looked almost as tired as she felt.

Yet she wanted to make love to him as much as he said he wanted to make love to her. She could feel the desire slowly building, but she wasn't going to push it to happen tonight. They still had tomorrow and tomorrow night. More than enough time before heading home. She was just happy that they were out of the entire mess with the Senator.

She brushed her teeth and crawled into the wonderful-feeling clean sheets, letting them soothe her almost as much as the hot water had done earlier.

Craig had just finished brushing his teeth and was coming out of the bathroom naked when there was a knock on the door.

He glanced at her and she shrugged. One-thirty in the morning wasn't a normal time for anyone to come knocking.

"Who is it? Craig shouted at the door, moving at it to check through the peephole.

"Room service," Bonnie heard a man's voice on the other side respond.

Craig looked through the hole in the door, then said, "We didn't order any room service."

"Yes, I know, sir," Bonnie heard. "This is from a friend. A surprise."

Something was bothering her about that voice. About all this, but she couldn't put her finger on it.

Craig glanced back at Bonnie and just shook his head. Then he shouted through the door. "Hold on a second."

"Who would send us something at this time of the night?" Bonnie asked Craig as he climbed into a pair of shorts and padded back toward the door.

"I'm betting on Hagar," Craig said. "Or the Senator."

Bonnie nodded. That was possible. The Senator was a kind-enough man to do something like this all the way from Washington D.C..

But still, there was something wrong here.

Craig opened the door and stood back as a man in a hotel uniform pushed a food cart into the room.

"Hello," the man said to Bonnie as she held the sheets up under her chin.

Bonnie felt a shock run through her. She knew that voice from...

Suddenly, just as Craig was about to let the door close, two other men burst in, both pointing pistols at Craig.

"What the...?" Craig said, backing away from the door with his hands raised.

Before Bonnie could even react, the man in the hotel uniform pulled out a pistol and leveled it at her, motioning for her to remain still.

She pulled the sheet up even farther over her breasts and stared at the man.

The guy just smiled in return.

The door closed behind the three armed gunmen with a resounding thud and Bonnie suddenly knew that she and Craig were far from out of this entire mess. In fact, they had just become part of the mess.

"I would suggest you both put some clothes on," the man in the hotel uniform said. "You're going for a ride to visit a friend." He smiled. "I told you it was a surprise."

Now Bonnie absolutely knew the voice. She would remember that voice anywhere. Standing in a hotel uniform with a gun pointed at her was the second man they had overheard on the golf course on Friday night.

She glanced at Craig, but he was staring at the two guns pointed at him.

"Let's go, people," the man said. "We honestly don't have all night."

Bonnie hadn't let another man see her nude since she married Craig, but at the moment it looked as if she didn't have much choice in the matter. She had no doubt this guy would shoot her without a second thought. And dying in this hotel room wasn't in her plans for the future.

She tossed the sheet aside and stood, moving over to where she had dropped her shorts and blouse when she had put on her swimming suit. With her back to the man, she dressed quickly.

By the time she turned around to again face the guns, Craig had on a golf shirt and was slipping on tennis shoes.

She retrieved her tennis shoes from near the bed and put them on as well.

When she stood, the man in the hotel uniform said, "Good. Now all three of us are going to walk down the hall and through the hotel lobby to a waiting limousine I have out front."

He pulled off the hotel uniform jacket and untucked his shirt to make himself look like a guest.

Craig glanced at Bonnie, but said nothing.

The man pointed his gun at Craig. "Detective, one false move in the hall or lobby and your pretty wife here will be the first to die, I promise you. My men and I have no problem firing in a public place. Chances are she will not be the only person to die. Am I understood?"

"Perfectly," Craig said.

"Good," the man said. He indicated they should go.

One of the gunmen opened the door and took up a position out in the hall, his gun inside a jacket pocket, but still very much in evidence.

Bonnie moved through the door beside Craig and walked beside him down the hall with the men following.

The ride down the elevator was long and uncomfortable, since Bonnie and Craig stood facing the door, the three men behind them. Bonnie could just imagine the three guns pointing at the small of her back. She didn't like the feeling at all.

The walk through the hotel lobby was just plain frightening. There had to be twenty people standing around or walking through the lobby. Couldn't they see what was happening?

It seemed that no one did.

There were no shouts or alarms and a few moments later they were out the front door, down the steps, and into the back of a waiting stretch limo.

The three men sat facing Bonnie and Craig. Two had their guns in their hands. The man clearly in charge just sat back and smiled.

Bonnie didn't feel like smiling back.

"Relax and enjoy the ride," the man said. "We don't have that far to go."

Neither Craig nor Bonnie said a word.

Bonnie had no idea why they were being taken and any question she might ask would only chance giving the man information he might not have. So she said nothing.

Outside the streets of Scottsdale flashed past, the night traffic very light on this early Monday morning.

Chapter Twenty-Two

Monday, April 10th
1:49 a.m.

CRAIG TRIED TO make sure he knew where they were, where they had turned, and what part of Scottsdale they were in. He wished he was more familiar with the area, but if needed, he might be able to retrace the steps from the hotel to the general area they were in now.

Maybe.

Their kidnappers sure seemed unconcerned that he was able to see where they were going. And that lack of concern bothered him. It usually meant that the kidnappers had no thoughts of ever letting them go.

The limo finally pulled over beside an open area, just short of a massive stone wall that towered twenty feet over the street and stretched for a least a half mile. Craig could see that there were a number of very large estates nearby, the biggest more than likely behind the wall. But right at this spot there was nothing but empty desert.

"Okay," the man said. "Time for a little talk."

He motioned for the two other gunmen to get out of the limo and then close the doors. When they did, he turned back to face Craig, smiling, his gun in his hand leveled on Bonnie's midsection.

"Just listen," the man said. "I have no desire to kill either of you. But make no mistake, I will if I have to."

Craig nodded and out of the corner of his eye he saw Bonnie do the same.

"First off, my name is not important. Charles Robins calls me Bill, so we'll just go with that."

Craig started at the name of Charles Robins. What was this guy up to anyway?

"I'll tell you this right up front," the man said, "Charles Robins hired me to stage an accident with Senator Knight so that Knight would not be able to vote later today in Washington on a piece of legislation that would hurt Robins."

Craig desperately wanted to tell this guy that he had failed, but knew that wouldn't be a good idea at this point. The guy would find out soon enough as it was.

The bigger question is why this guy was telling them all this information?

"I have put tapes of my conversations with Mr. Robins in a locker at the train station." The man flipped Bonnie the key.

She was so surprised that she almost didn't catch it.

"The locker number is on the key. If you get out of this alive, that's the key to the locker."

Craig, in all his years of police work, had never been this confused before. "So why are you telling us this?" Craig asked.

The guy laughed. "I suppose this all does seem a little odd to a police detective used to criminals trying to cover their guilt instead of admit it."

"A little," Craig said, as sarcastically as he could.

The man snickered. "Trust me, Detective, I will never be caught for this crime."

Now Craig understood. "But you want Charles Robins to be, is that it?"

"Exactly," the man said.

"Why?" Bonnie asked.

"Because the man wouldn't pay me what we agreed he should pay me for the work I did."

Now it was Craig's turn to laugh. "The old saying comes back to bite you, huh?"

The guy smiled at Craig. "You are right, detective. No honor among thieves is how the saying goes. But I keep my word and I expect others to do the same. Charles Robins did not."

"And now he must pay the price," Bonnie said. "Is that it?"

"Exactly," the man said.

"So couldn't you have just called the police, left the tape, and ran like hell," Craig asked. "Why go through all the problems of kidnapping us?"

"For one I would have never had the pleasure of seeing your fine wife here without clothes on."

Beside him Craig could feel Bonnie tighten even more, but she said nothing and didn't move.

"Secondly," the man said, going on, "Charles Robins is an idiot and I want to make sure he is so deep into this mess that no amount of money will buy his way out."

"And that's where we come in," Craig said. "Right?"

"Exactly," the man said. "Let's go."

With that he opened the door, and with the point of his gun, indicated that they should get out of the limo.

Craig climbed out with Bonnie behind him, followed by the man.

Outside a third man had joined the other two. He was very large and muscled, with a military posture and build. He was perfectly proportioned and as Craig got closer he realized the guy had to be at least six-four.

The big man nodded to the one who had been talking to them in the limo, then turned to the other two guards. "Tie their hands behind their backs."

Each guard did as he was told.

Craig could feel the rope being pulled painfully tight as he attempted to keep his wrists apart and his muscles flexed.

"Ow!" Bonnie said, glancing back at the guy behind her. "Not so damned tight. I might need those hands again."

After they were finished being tied, the tall man turned to the guards. "Take our two prisoners to Mr. Robins' study, then have him awakened. Give him this note."

The big man handed the guard behind Craig a piece of paper.

"Through the front gate, sir?" the guard asked.

"Does it matter to you?" the large man demanded, moving up into the guard's face. "Or would you like me to do it and find someone to take your place?"

The big man towered over both Craig and the guard.

Craig could hear the guard swallow behind him.

"No, sir," the guard said, clearly afraid of the big man.

Smart thinking.

Craig wouldn't want to tangle with the guy either.

"Now follow orders," the big man said. "I have another task to complete."

The guard pushed Craig down the street while the other shoved Bonnie ahead of him.

After about twenty steps Craig glanced back over his shoulder. The man they had overheard on the fairway on Friday, the man who had told them he was hired to complete the plot against the Senator, was climbing back into the limo with the larger man. Both were laughing.

That made Craig shiver.

Craig looked ahead at the distant front gate to what must be Charles Robins' walled estate. And just to the right, sitting peacefully on the street, was the white van Craig knew held the FBI observers. Maxwell was going to go nuts when he saw this on tape.

If Craig had had his hands free, he would have waved as they passed.

And that was exactly what the guy who had kidnapped them had wanted.

He and Bonnie were bait.

The FBI was the weapon.

And the target was Charles Robins.

Craig had a feeling that getting him and Bonnie out of this alive was going to take more luck than he wanted to admit.

CHAPTER TWENTY-THREE

Monday, April 10th
2:17 a.m.

CHARLES ROBINS DIDN'T much like getting awakened in the middle of his sleep. And tonight was no exception.

Yet the guard didn't seem to want to let it go.

"I'm sorry, sir," the guard said, his voice seeming to blare over the private intercom. "It is important that you come to your study at once."

"I'll be right there," Robins said. He crawled out of bed slowly, rubbing his face. Screw going right there. He was in charge here, and he'd get down there in his own damned time.

It took him ten minutes to put on clothes, use the bathroom, and pour himself a glass of juice before he finally went down the private stairs to his office.

He expected Grant to be there with some problem, standing at attention in front of his desk like he always did. But instead he saw two guards with a tied up man and woman. Both the man and the woman were in shorts.

"What's this all about?" he demanded.

"Charles Robins, I presume," the tied man said.

"And just who the hell are you?" Robins asked.

"I'm Detective Frakes," the guy said, smiling. He nodded at the woman beside him. "This is Officer Stanley. We're both with the Seattle police department."

Robins felt his stomach clamp up into a tight ball. These were the two who had been playing with Senator Knight all weekend. What in the hell were they doing here?

"What were you two trying to do, break in to my estate?"

The man shook his head no. "I'm afraid your men came and got us from our hotel room bed."

Charles glared at the guard. "Is that true?"

"Yes, sir," the guard said.

Charles just stared at the guard, not really believing what he had been told. His men had kidnapped two cops, the same two who had been playing for two days with Senator Knight, from their hotel room and brought them to his study.

"Why would you do that?" Charles almost screamed. "Where's Grant?"

Charles stared at one guard, then the other.

The guard behind the tied-up detective stepped forward. "Grant told me to give you this note, sir,"

"Note?" Charles asked. "I don't want any note. I want to talk to him. Now!"

The guard only shook and looked afraid, so Robins took the note and opened it.

Dear Charles,
 Since you saw fit to short me one-half-million dol-
lars for the job you hired me to do on Senator Knight, I
felt you deserved something for my troubles.
 Enjoy,
 Bill

Underneath the first note there was a second hand-scrawled note in another color pen. It said:

Dear Mr. Robins,
 I cannot work for a man who would hurt a Sena-
tor and kidnap fellow police officers. I quit.
 Sincerely,
 Grant

"Damn, damn, damn," Charles said, reading the notes over again. There was no chance at all of being able to show this note to anyone. He stopped and looked up at the guard. "You said Grant gave you this note?"

"Yes, sir," the guard said.

"Was there another man with Grant when he gave it to you?"

"Yes, sir," the guard said. "A man who called himself Bill."

Suddenly the past few years were all making sense. It was no wonder this Bill person could get into the estate through the security so easily every time he was called. He and Grant, his chief of security, had been working together all this time.

And now the guy had made Charles look as if he had ordered the kidnapping of these two police officers. And that might be enough to tie him to what happened to Senator Knight. With the motive, it was more than enough, that was for sure.

Charles moved over and sat down behind his desk, trying to clear his mind.

He had to figure out what to do next.

And no option looked good.

"Sir?" the guard asked, "what do I do with the prisoners?"

Charles glanced at the two cops, then shook his head. "Put them in a closet and guard them until I decide what to do next."

"But sir," the guard said, "the FBI knows they are in here."

"Of course they do," Charles said. "Don't you think I know that? Now do as I say. And for god's sake, don't hurt them."

As the two were being led out Charles drank his juice as calmly as he could. He hadn't thought of the FBI. The man named Bill had set a perfect trap.

Charles leaned back and looked around at his beautiful study. With the Senator not voting tomorrow, he was going to keep control of his fortune. And that meant he could afford the expensive attorneys who could get him off this hook.

He would blame Grant and the man named Bill as getting greedy, as taking too much control in his problems. His lawyers would get him off as a man who let his employees take too much control.

He could feel the plan starting to form. In a few hours he would turn over the two detectives personally, claiming he just had learned about the plan.

If he worked it right, with enough spin and good enough attorneys, he might just come out of this all right.

CHAPTER TWENTY-FOUR

Monday, April 10th
2:36 a.m.

THE GUARDS SHOVED them both into a small hall closet and closed the door, plunging them into darkness.

Bonnie bumped against Craig and then used the right wall of the closet to get her balance. The ropes around her wrists had become painful about ten minutes after they had been put on, and now they were just a dull ache. From what she saw before they were shoved inside, the closet had a few coats hanging in it, all on wooden hangers. Nothing more.

"You all right?" Craig whispered.

"Fine," she whispered back, keeping her voice soft enough so that no one outside the closet could hear. "Just completely confused."

She still couldn't believe what had happened to them.

Taken from their hotel room by a man who wanted to frame another man. Then told about it.

It was just too weird.

"Seems like we're pawns in a game between murderers," Craig said, his voice low and coming out of the darkness. "I sure don't much like that idea."

"I couldn't agree more," she said. "That Charles Robins gives me the creeps."

"Slime describes him just fine," Craig said.

"So what do you think is going to happen next?" Bonnie asked. "You think the FBI guys saw us?"

"They would have had to be asleep to miss us," Craig said.

"It's getting lighter in here," Bonnie said.

Her eyes were adjusting to the dim light coming through under the door and around the cracks in the casing. She could barely see the outline of Craig leaning against the other wall a foot or so from her.

"It is," Craig said. "And we have to be ready for anything that's going to happen next. How tight are your ropes?"

"Tight," she said. "But I can still move my fingers."

"So can I," he said. "You want to try untying mine first?"

"Sure," she said, turning her back to him. "Let me get into a stable position and you put your ropes in my hands."

"Good idea," he said.

Bonnie leaned forward, head against the wall for balance. Behind her she could feel Craig's hands against hers. Then he lowered his hands so that her fingers were on the ropes around his wrists.

The knots felt tight and it took her a moment to find a place to even try to start working the knot loose.

Then she noticed that Craig's fingers were between her legs, against her crotch because of how she was leaning forward.

She moved her butt slightly. "This could be more fun than I thought."

He laughed lightly and moved his fingers against the seam of her shorts, keeping his wrists still so she could work on the knot.

She could feel that she was making a little progress, but not much. "Can you move your wrists to your right slightly, and turn them to the left?"

"Sure," he said. As he moved to the right he slipped one finger under the leg of her shorts and pulled up as he twisted his wrists to the left.

That put two of his fingers right up against her bare flesh. She made herself focus on untying the knot.

"No underwear," he whispered. "Nice."

His fingers moved back and forth.

She tried to focus on the knot, and it seemed to be coming free slowly, but Craig's fingers were distracting her.

"That feels wonderful," she said softly. "But you're not helping me get you untied."

His fingers stopped. She desperately wanted to push back against them, but the fear of losing the progress she made on the knot stopped her.

She forced herself to work at the rope, ignoring the sense of his touch against her crotch.

What seemed like an eternity later she said, "I think I've almost got it."

His fingers slid a little farther along her crotch.

"I'd agree with that," he said, the humor clear in his voice even in the dark.

"You keep that up and I'm never going to get this untied," she said.

"Nothing but promises," he said, laughing as his fingers moved a little again and then stopped. The movement sent chills through her, and small ripples of pleasure swirling in her stomach.

She focused on the knot, finally pulling it free.

"Got it," she said.

"Nice job," he said. "Stay put and I'll untie you."

She could feel his hands working on the ropes on her wrists, and as he did she moved her butt back against his crotch.

"Now you're the one slowing down this process," he said.

"Well then hurry up and get me untied," she said, moving her butt slowly back and forth. She loved teasing him, just as he loved teasing her.

Finally she felt the wonderful relief of the ropes coming off. She stood up and rubbed her wrists, trying to get circulation back through them. She had no doubt she was going to have bruises there for weeks.

"Now what?" she asked.

Craig kissed her quickly, then turned and pulled one of the wooden hangers off the bar. He slapped it against his hand. "Get one and let's see if we can get out of here."

She did as he suggested, the weight of the hanger in her hands not giving her any reassurance at all.

Craig turned and carefully tried the door handle. It was locked and as he tried to turn it, the knob rattled.

"You two stay quiet in there," a guards voice came from the other side of the door, loud and very, very close. "You'll be let out soon enough."

"Shit," Craig whispered.

Bonnie turned and put the hanger back on the hook, then sat down on the floor, her back against the back wall of the closet. They weren't getting out of this closet any time soon.

She watched as Craig gave the closet one more close inspection and then sat down beside her.

"What a way to spend a vacation," she whispered.

"As long as it's with you," Craig said, "I'd spend it locked in a closet."

"We are locked in a closet," she said.

"Oh," was all he said.

CHAPTER TWENTY-FIVE

Monday, April 10th
3:10 a.m.

MAXWELL LOOKED AT the rumpled and very tired Hagar as he staggered into the police station. A couple other night-shift detectives laughed, but no one said anything.

"This had better be damned good," Hagar said. "I was dreaming about swimming naked with a dozen women when you so rudely woke me up."

Maxwell laughed. "No wonder you look so tired." He pointed at the screen of a monitor sitting on a desk and punched play. He had watched these images a dozen times over the last ten minutes and still couldn't figure out exactly what they meant.

Hagar frowned. The image showed a tall wall and some people coming down the street toward the camera.

"The Robins estate," Maxwell said. "Filmed less than an hour ago."

"I know where it's at," Hagar said, "but who are the people?"

"Wait," Maxwell said.

On screen the images of the people became clearer and clearer.

"Holy shit, you're kidding?"

"I'm not," Maxwell said. "That's Bonnie and Craig, their hands tied, being led into the Robins estate by two of Robins' goons. I checked their room and they are not there."

"Robins kidnapped them?" Hagar almost shouted as the film showed Bonnie and Craig being walked right through the front gate. "Why the hell would he do that?"

"I don't know the answer to that question," Maxwell said, "but they haven't come out of there yet."

Hagar shook his head. "Didn't they know your van was there filming everything?"

"I guess not," Maxwell said. "Or I doubt they would have taken them in this way."

Hagar glanced at Maxwell. "Are you thinking what I think you are thinking? You want to go in after them?"

Maxwell nodded. "I've got agents flying up here from Tucson and down from Vegas. I can have a force of over thirty men ready to roll in forty minutes."

"And you think Bonnie and Craig are still alive in there?" Hagar asked.

"At the moment I do," Maxwell said, "but the longer we wait, the less chance I give them. And I give them no chance when Robins discovers they helped trick him with the Senator."

"Damn, you're right," Hagar said. He rewound the film again quickly and watched them walk past the truck and through the main gate.

To Maxwell there was no doubt both Craig and Bonnie were tied and being led at gunpoint.

"Robins might have over fifty men in there," Hagar said, "and from what I've observed about those men, they aren't afraid to defend that place."

"I assumed as much," Maxwell said. "That's why we need to work together on this."

Hagar just stared at him for a moment, then said, "You're nuts, you know that?"

Maxwell nodded.

"Shit, shit, shit!" Hagar said, turning from Maxwell and picking up the phone.

Ten minutes later Hagar had permission to work with the FBI from the Chief of Police.

Thirty minutes later Hagar had a force of over fifty men, including a SWAT team from Phoenix, staged at different locations around the Robins estate, armed and ready to go when the order was given.

Maxwell knew that if this turned into a gunfight, it was going to go down poorly. Their best bet was to try to talk their way in and disarm guards as they went.

Hagar was convinced that there was going to be no talking their way inside those walls. He had calls out for even more help to stand ready. He told Maxwell that if this didn't turn out to be the Alamo west, he'd be surprised.

That was the last thing Maxwell wanted to have happen. But inside those walls were two kidnapped cops and a man they suspected of trying to kill a United States Senator. He had no other choice.

They had to go in.

CHAPTER TWENTY-SIX

Monday, April 10th
4:03 a.m.

BONNIE HAD DOZED lightly for most of the past half hour, and Craig had let her. The closet had gotten cold and Bonnie had pulled down one of the expensive wool coats that hung in there to use as a cover. And she was using Craig as a pillow, something he didn't mind at all.

Craig had talked her into closing her eyes for a short time. There was just no point in both of them trying to stay alert. There wasn't much they could do until Robins decided to let them out. Unless they wanted to take a chance on getting shot trying to escape, and at the moment Craig didn't much like that idea.

So until something happened, they sat on the floor, in the dark, and waited.

Craig guessed that at least an hour or more had gone by since Robins had tossed them into the closet. And if that was the case, they were getting closer and closer to the Senator's press conference in Washington. Craig had no desire to still be Robins' prisoner when he discovered the Senator was still healthy and voting.

A slight snoring noise rumbled the closet and Craig eased Bonnie sideways. Usually she didn't snore, but considering how tired she was, and the circumstances, it was understandable.

Bonnie mumbled and cuddled against his side as the snoring sound happened again. He shook her lightly, then when her eyes popped open he whispered, "Shhh, listen."

The snoring sound came again.

She sat upright in the darkness, then leaned toward him and whispered, "The guard's asleep."

"That's what I thought," Craig said.

"Think we can break that lock open?" she asked, her voice barely audible.

"Yeah," he said, silently standing and moving his legs to make sure the circulation hadn't left them. He had taken out other locks much stronger than the one on this closet door. And from the sounds of the snoring, the guard was leaning against the door. So the break-out would have to be strong enough to snap the lock and shove the guard aside at the same time. If the wood in the door held, it would work.

"What do you want me to do?" Bonnie asked.

"Be ready to hit the guy on the head with one of those wooden hangers," Craig whispered.

The snoring stopped for an instant, the guy shifted against the door, moving more away from the lock, then a moment later the snoring started again.

Craig let out the breath he had been holding. "Ready?"

"As I'll ever be," Bonnie whispered.

Craig braced himself against the back wall of the closet. It was just a little too far from the door to give him the best force on his kick. He used both hands to lightly pull on the hanger bar. It seemed very solid and secure in place. It would hold his weight long enough for him to kick the door open, he was sure.

He leaned toward Bonnie and whispered, "Here we go."

"Careful," she whispered back.

"You too," he said.

He put himself in position directly behind the door's handle, then with two deep breaths, he pulled himself up on the bar and with all the force he could manage in both legs, kicked the door with both feet.

It smashed open like it hadn't even been latched.

Bonnie was through the door before he could even let go of the bar.

The guard had been shoved head over heels away from the door by the force of Craig's kicks.

Bonnie was around the open door and over the guard by the time the guy even started to get up. One very hard smack against the side of the head with the wooden hanger and the guy went back to sleep.

"He's going to have one massive headache when he wakes up," Bonnie said, smiling at her husband.

"Remind me to never get you mad at me."

Craig grabbed the guy's rifle, a semi-automatic with a dozen rounds in the clip. The guy had one in the chamber, ready to fire.

Bonnie dug around in the guard's pockets and pulled out two more clips for the rifle and a 44 caliber pistol with extra rounds. Then she took an earplug from the guard's ear and a small communications device from his front pocket of his vest.

She handed the communication equipment to Craig.

"Better find out what his name is," Craig said, "so we can answer a call to him."

Bonnie quickly flipped the guy over and dug his wallet out of his back pocket. She flipped it open and then snorted. "Dwight. His name is Dwight."

A security guard named Dwight. No wonder he had fallen asleep.

She stuck the wallet back in the guy's pants and stood.

"Keep watch," he said.

He grabbed the guard and pulled him back into the closet, then tied his hands and feet with the rope they had been tied with.

The closet door, with a little work, almost looked like nothing had happened to it by the time Craig got it closed again.

"Now what?" Bonnie asked.

Craig glanced down the corridor. There was a security camera trained on the corner about fifty feet away. And another one in the other direction down the hall. It looked like they were between them at least.

"There's got to be a major security system in this place, as well as at least twenty guards, if not a lot more," he said. He pointed at the cameras as he stuck the earplug in his ear.

"Damn," she said, "we move from here at all and they'll know we've escaped."

"So when we do move, we make the best of it," Craig said, "and move fast."

"Until then we wait here?" Bonnie asked.

In his ear Craig could hear the sudden excited talking of the front guards, as well as others along the perimeter of the estate. They were all reporting in that a large number of police had suddenly moved up into position.

"Exactly," he said, smiling at her. "But I don't think we're going to have to wait long. We're about to have the cavalry come to the rescue."

CHAPTER TWENTY-SEVEN

Monday, April 10th
4:27 a.m.

"ARE WE READY?" Maxwell asked Hagar.

"My people are," Hagar said, nodding as he listened to the last of status reports in his ear.

"So are mine," Maxwell said. "Let's do it."

Maxwell picked up a bullhorn as the two of them stepped around the police car and walked ten feet out into the middle of the road in front of the main gate of the Robins estate. Above them the stars were shining and the air was crisp and almost cold. Maxwell could see a dozen men in different positions inside the gate, guns all at rest. As long as they stayed that way, everything would be fine.

"Attention. This is the FBI," Maxwell shouted through the bull-horn, his voice echoing over the estate and into the rock hills behind it. "Open the gates and throw down your weapons. You are completely surrounded."

Nothing.

He knew that he had the horn set loud enough that anyone inside the buildings beyond those wall would be able to hear him as well. He would give good old Robins a moment to think about things, and then try again.

The silence of the late desert night seemed intense as Maxwell and Hagar waited. Inside the gate no one moved.

"This is the FBI!" Maxwell repeated through the horn. "Throw down your weapons and come out."

Again the silence seemed to crawl down over him like a giant bug trying to smother him. He could feel his own heart beating and the fear choking him. But he stood there, in the middle of the road, and waited for a response.

Then through the gate there was movement, but it took Maxwell a fraction of a second to realize it was the wrong kind of movement. One of the men just inside the gate to the right was raising his gun.

Another behind him was doing the same.

"Get down!" Hagar shouted and turned to get to cover.

Maxwell spun and ran, the ten steps between him and the shelter of the patrol car seemingly a thousand yards.

The air suddenly echoed with the sounds of gunfire. For an instant it was only a few shots, all coming from beyond the walls, then there was more and more until it was impossible to tell how many, as if strings of firecrackers were being shot off in a closed space.

Maxwell's agents were now returning fire, trying to cover him as he and Hagar got to shelter.

A bullet smashed into the car just beyond him.

Close!

Way too damned close!

He tried to dive for the shelter of the front fender of the car.

He didn't make it.

The burning feeling of the bullet cutting through the flesh of his back wasn't as bad as he expected. But the impact flipped him completely over, smashing him to the concrete. The fall hurt like hell, and he banged his head, knocking him into blackness for a moment.

He came to in time to feel Hagar's hands grab him and drag him beyond the car and over into a shallow ditch beside the road.

There was no pain.

That surprised him.

He just couldn't move.

That also surprised him.

He should feel pain, he should be able to move. It was as if the wind had been knocked out of him and all his energy taken.

"Damn!" Hagar said. "Officer down here!"

Two other men swarmed into the ditch beside him as the gun battle continued, the quiet of the night now a continuous roar of explosions.

Maxwell noted it all like watching it from a distance. For some reason he knew that things were not going well, but a part of him just no longer cared.

"Hang in there," Hagar yelled to him, but it was like the cop was shouting down a long tunnel.

Maxwell felt himself smile.

He had been shot and it hadn't really hurt.

And now he was going to die. He knew that as clearly as he had known anything in his life.

And that was all right as well.

This experience was not at all what he had expected death to feel like.

He looked up at the pained expression on Hagar's face and knew exactly what the cop wanted him to say.

How he knew, he wasn't sure, but he just knew.

He used one hand to pull Hagar down closer, then in his ear he said, "Get the damned son-of-a-bitch for me, would you?"

"I will," Hagar said.

Maxwell really didn't care, but he knew that Hagar did. And if the situation was reversed, Hagar would have said it for him as well.

Maxwell felt he was floating now, sort of watching what was happening to him like an observer from a distance. He was both in his body and watching them around his body.

There was no pain.

Just a wonderful sense of floating.

"Maxwell!"

The voice sort of pulled at him, but he ignored it. He liked the floating.

"Maxwell!" Hagar shouted. "Maxwell, stay with us!"

But Maxwell could see no point in staying.

And with that he died.

CHAPTER TWENTY-EIGHT

Monday, April 10th
4:32 a.m.

CRAIG WAS STUNNED when the shooting began.

"What the hell is going on?" Bonnie asked, clearly as afraid and as stunned as he was. They had both heard Maxwell tell Robins' men to lay down their guns and come out. At the time the voice had cheered them.

Then in his ear Craig had heard the command come from Robins directly. "Keep the FBI out at all costs."

A moment later the shooting had started.

"The stupid ass ordered them to fight the FBI," Craig said, shaking his head in amazement. "What the hell is he thinking?"

"Maybe that's our problem," Bonnie said. "We keep expecting the man to think."

"Well, we need to stop this," Craig said. "There's a lot of good men out there getting fired on."

"And just two of us in here," Bonnie said. "You got any smart ideas?"

"Sure," Craig said. "We capture the head of this snake and tell him to shut things down."

Bonnie nodded and glanced down the hall. "I can remember how to get back to his study, but we're going to have to do it fast and without stopping."

"Agreed," Craig said. "I'll take the lead and you cover my back."

She pinched his butt. "I'll make sure this doesn't get shot off if you take care of that guy in front."

"Deal," he said.

Outside the gunfire was becoming even more intense. It was a war out there and unless it stopped quickly a lot of people were going to get hurt or killed.

He kissed her and then turned and headed down the hall, knowing she was right behind him.

At that moment what he really wanted was to lock them both in a closet and only come out when the shooting was over, but he knew neither one of them could do that.

They were cops. It was their lives.

And right now a lot of other cops were getting shot at. If they had the best chance of stopping it, they needed to take it.

They had to take it.

With the rifle leveled and ready to fire he went around the first corner under the camera. There was no one in the hallway.

He kept moving at a near run.

Bonnie stayed close behind, the sound of her footsteps almost matching his. In about fifty paces the hallway opened up into a wide foyer with plants on one side and a door leading outside to the right.

The door into Robins' study was to the left and down another short hallway.

There was a guard poised, facing the exterior door, as if waiting for someone to come through.

Craig shouted, "Drop the gun!"

The guard was too stupid for words.

Instead of dropping the gun he spun and tried to fire.

Craig cut him down with a short blast, almost ripping the guard in half with the tight pattern of his bullets.

"To the left!" Bonnie said behind him and Craig headed that way.

Ahead of him a guard poked his head out of a door and Craig fired through the edge of the door and wood of the wall, aiming at where the man's midsection would be.

The guy jerked and fell out into the hallway, clearly dead. Any good cop knew that the wood and plasterboard of regular house walls didn't stop most bullets. This guy clearly had watched too much television thinking he was safe behind that door.

"Grab his rifle," Craig said as he checked the room the guard had been in for anyone else, and then moved on down the hall.

Robins' study was two more doors away.

Bonnie grabbed the rifle and kept guard behind him as Craig stared at that office door.

There was no doubt that there was someone on the other side of it waiting for him to come through.

And the minute he did, he was dead.

He didn't want to be dead just yet.

But there was a guy here that already had that distinction, and wouldn't mind a few more holes, Craig figured.

Craig went back and picked up the guy he had just killed, keeping the rifle in one hand as he did it. The dead guy wasn't that heavy, or the adrenaline in Craig's body was working overtime.

The guy's blood got on his hands, but Craig ignored it.

"Get on the floor and cover me," he said to his wife and rushed at the study door, the guy's body a shield ahead of him.

Just before he reached the door he tossed the body as hard as he could, using his running momentum to get the body to hit the door halfway up and at a good speed.

Then Craig dropped to the carpet, rifle pointed ahead.

The body smashed open the study door and was instantly peppered with bullets, making the dead man jerk and flip his arms as he dropped.

Craig had his gun up and firing before the body was out of the way.

Almost instantly the gunfire from inside the study stopped. A moment later there was the sound of a gun hitting the floor.

Craig dove over the dead man and rolled, coming up with his rifle facing Charles Robins' scared face and his shaking hand that was holding a small pistol.

To Robins' right was the guard who had been firing, now slumped in, and bleeding all over, an expensive leather chair.

"I would suggest you drop that gun now," Bonnie said, moving to cover her husband. "I would love to pull this trigger and blow those tiny brains of yours all over your desk."

Charles glanced at her, then dropped his gun like it was suddenly too hot to hold.

Craig used the barrel of his rifle to kick the gun onto the floor.

"Now," he said to Robins, "tell your men to drop their weapons and surrender."

Robins hesitated until Craig raised his rifle and pointed it at the man's head. Then Robins picked up a small communications unit and said, "Attention. This is Robins. Drop your weapons now. Cease fire."

Slowly the noise of gunfire died off, replaced by a wonderful silence filled only by distant sirens.

"Tell them to put their hands on their heads and walk toward the nearest cop until told otherwise," Craig said.

Robins hesitated.

"Oh, please let me shoot him," Bonnie said, moving up and putting her gun against the side of his head.

"Oh, I kind of like this side of you," Craig said, smiling at her.

"Let me pull the trigger and see how hot it gets me," she said, winking at him.

Robins instantly moved to do as Craig had ordered, repeating his words exactly. He clearly believed Bonnie would kill him.

"Now what?" Robins asked as he finished.

"Now we shoot you," Bonnie said, raising her gun again.

"She's just kidding," Craig said, smiling at the sick look on Robins' face. "But I won't hesitate. So come on out from behind there and sit at the feet of your dead man there."

Robins did as Craig told him until he stood over his dead guard. Then he turned and shook his head. "I can't do that."

"You caused his death," Craig said. "Seems you owe him a little company. Now sit down."

Craig jammed his rifle into Robins' chest and the man dropped to the floor.

Craig took the dead man's arms and placed them around Robins' neck, as if the man was giving his boss a hug from behind. Blood dripped down the front of Robins' shirt from the man's hand.

"Now isn't that sweet?" Bonnie asked Craig.

Craig couldn't think of a better thing to have happen to the man who wanted Senator Knight dead. And who had ordered his men to fire on police.

Charles Robins looked as if he might throw up at any minute, but with Bonnie's rifle leveled on his chest, he didn't move.

Ten minutes later Hagar and a dozen others swarmed into the room. Once they saw that Craig and Bonnie had it under control, they stopped and all but two of them moved off to finish checking the house.

"I was wondering why they suddenly stopped firing and gave up," Hagar said.

Craig pointed at where Robins still sat with the dead guard's arms around his neck. "He just needed a little convincing is all. And Bonnie is a real good convincer."

Craig smiled at his wife as she nodded her thanks.

"Does he know about Senator Knight's press conference yet?" Hagar asked.

"When is that scheduled?" Bonnie asked, smiling at the startled look from Robins.

"Eight eastern time," Hagar said. "Just about any moment now."

"Well," Craig said, "Bonnie turn it on while someone reads Mr. Robins his rights."

Hagar got down on one knee in front of Robins, and without moving the dead man's arms off the guy's shoulders, read Charles Robins his rights.

A moment later, on CNN, the serious face of Senator Knight appeared and began to talk.

For a short moment Charles Robins just stared at the screen, then slowly he closed his eyes.

"Ain't justice wonderful?" Craig asked, listening as Senator Knight thanked him and Bonnie for saving his life.

CHAPTER TWENTY-NINE

Monday, April 10th
6:36 a.m.

THE LIMO PULLED through the gate and out onto the tarmac of the Scottsdale airport, stopping beside the two private jets just as the sun was breaking over the hills to the east. A moment later the man Charles Robins called Bill finished his last phone call. He hung up the phone, then flipped closed the laptop computer he had been holding on his lap.

"Well?" Grant asked.

Bill looked across the private area of the limo at his old friend Grant and smiled.

"Done?" Grant asked.

"Done," Bill said. "We've just moved over sixty-seven million of Charles Robins' company's money to varied accounts, and then on to other numbered accounts. It will be moved automatically another hundred times, in varied amounts, before it finally settles in our accounts."

"As always no one can trace it?" Grant asked.

"Trust me," Bill said, "if someone does try to trace it, it will look like Charles did it himself. And the money will be gone. Hell, it will take a team of auditors years to find everything that's missing."

Grant laughed, the sound filling the limo. "The man was just too stupid for words."

"That he was. And I must say, it was a pleasure taking him for every penny."

"It almost makes taking orders from the idiot for four years worth it."

"Sixty-seven million?" Bill said, laughing. "I'd say that was worth it. You got us access to everything the man owned, every password, every account. And the guy let you." Bill shook his head at the craziness of it all.

Grant laughed, his big frame shaking. "Sure hope those two nice cops from Seattle got out of that firefight alive. She was a looker."

"I'm sure they did," Bill said. "They were smart enough to save the Senator, they're smart enough to get out of Robins' house, I'm sure."

"I sure wanted to tell old Robins about Senator Knight being just fine in Washington, D.C.," Grant said, laughing.

"If he doesn't know by now," Bill said, "he will shortly."

The two men laughed again and climbed out of the limo.

Bill looked at the two planes. One jet waited for him, the other for Grant. They were headed in two different directions.

In a matter of hours they would both be far out of the reach of Charles Robins and the FBI. In a matter of days they would both have new identities and enough money to last a very long time.

"Well, friend," Grant said, shaking his hand. "When will I see you again?"

"Oh, a year or so. As soon as I find another sucker like Robins. I'll be in touch."

"Take your time," Grant said. "I think I've got enough to last for a few years."

The man who had been called Bill laughed.

They let go of the handshake and turned for their jets.

It was the third time they had done this to a stupid, greedy businessman like Robins. They both knew it wouldn't be the last. They enjoyed the score too much. It made life worth living for both of them.

Bill's jet left the runway first, followed a minute later by Grant's.

In the air one jet turned west, the other south.

EPILOGUE

Friday, April 14th
10:12 p.m.

MONDAY HAD TURNED into a day from hell for both of them. Bonnie could not remember a day like it before. They had had no sleep and millions of questions to answer, forms to fill out, details to go over.

And all while trying to understand that Maxwell had been killed.

Bonnie found his death almost impossible to believe for some reason. The guy seemed like he always had everything under control. But clearly he had made one mistake, and that was walking into the line of fire of that estate's front gate.

Hagar had told them that he was lucky to get back when the firing started.

Bonnie still hadn't believed Maxwell was dead until the funeral on Thursday. Then finally she had allowed herself to cry for the man she had only known a short time.

By six in the evening on Monday they had been allowed to return to their hotel room for a shower and change of clothes.

But Hagar had had a car bring them right back to the station.

By midnight Monday they had finished almost everything that needed to be done immediately, and were allowed to go back to the hotel to sleep.

By eight the next morning they were back at the station.

The hearings and interviews seemed to stretch forever. Over and over again, both together and separately, Bonnie and Craig had answered questions about what had happened the entire weekend.

All day Tuesday, all day Wednesday, after Maxwell's funeral on Thursday, and then even more questions on Friday morning.

Finally, Friday afternoon they had been set free. Bonnie had felt numb and more tired than she had felt in years.

On Wednesday, Charles Robins had been arraigned on more counts than Bonnie believed was possible to charge one man with. And fifty-six of his men were under charges of attempted murder, murder, and so on. Besides Maxwell, ten others had died, all Robins' men. Ten cops and two FBI agents had been wounded, but only one seriously.

The firefight, combined with Senator Knight's sudden appearance in Washington, made all the national news and created a massive media stir around the police headquarters in Scottsdale that didn't die off until Thursday.

Somewhere in the middle of Monday afternoon, Bonnie remembered talking to her boss in Seattle, telling her they wouldn't be back for at least a week. Her boss completely understood.

Now it was Friday again. One week after they had first arrived for a weekend golf tournament. They had both taken naps in the afternoon and got out on the putting green and practiced for a few hours after dinner. But neither of their hearts were into playing golf.

As it was getting dark, Craig had suggested they go for a walk.

One week from the time they went for that first walk and overheard a conversation that changed a lot of lives.

"You sure you want to?" Bonnie asked, smiling at her husband. "You remember what happened last time we did that?"

"Sex?" he asked. "I remember sex on warm grass under bright stars."

She took his hand. "I think there's a rock out there with our name on it."

They strolled silently along the dark path.

She forced herself to not think about the events of the week. It was almost impossible to do, but somehow she wanted to get back to that feeling of just walking in the dark, enjoying Craig's company, and thinking about making love.

He held her hand and every so often would squeeze it.

But he said nothing either.

Seemingly, much faster than the first time they had made the walk in the dark, they reached the big rock.

Bonnie pulled him off the path and out onto the grass of the fairway.

She let go of his hand, kicked her shoes off, and laid down, enjoying the feeling of the warm grass against her skin.

They were both numb and she knew it, but somehow they had to come back to what they had together, put the week behind them and start new again.

She watched as he stood over her, his shape outlined against the stars.

"What are you thinking?" she asked, her voice sounding louder than she had expected in the night.

"Just how beautiful you are," he said.

"Really?" she asked, smiling up at him.

"Really," he said.

"And nothing else?" she asked.

"Just that you have too many clothes on for such a warm night."

She laughed, raised her hips and slid her shorts down and off her legs.

"How's that?"

"Better," he said, still just standing over her.

She sat up slightly and pulled her top over her head.

"Better," he said again.

She unhooked her bra and took it off.

"Getting close," he said.

She slid her panties off her legs and tossed them away.

"Perfect," he said.

She stood and gave him a long, hard kiss, then pushed him down onto the ground. "Now who has too many clothes on?"

They went through the same routine until he was nude and lying under her spread feet.

"I love this view," he said, staring up at her.

"Things don't look so bad from here," she said.

They stayed like that for a moment, then slowly she eased down on top of him, letting him hold her, letting him make love to her.

Finally, things were again right in the world.

They were together and that was all that mattered.

Be the first to know!

Just sign up for the Dean Wesley Smith newsletter, and keep up with the latest news, releases and so much more—even the occasional giveaway.

To sign up, go to deanwesleysmith.com.

But wait! There's more. Sign up for the WMG Publishing newsletter, too, and get the latest news and releases from all of the WMG authors and lines, including Kristine Kathryn Rusch, Kristine Grayson, Kris Nelscott, *Fiction River: An Original Anthology Magazine, Smith's Monthly,* and so much more.

Just go to wmgpublishing.com and click on Newsletter.

USA TODAY BESTSELLING AUTHOR
DEAN WESLEY
SMITH

A DOC HILL THRILLER

DEAD
MONEY

"[An] exhilarating political poker thriller."
— Midwest Book Reviews

If you enjoyed *An Easy Shot,* you might also enjoy the first book in the Doc Hill thriller series, *Dead Money,* available now from your favorite bookseller. Turn the page for a sample chapter.

PROLOGUE

SILENCE.

Silence, the absolute worst thing a pilot can experience at seven thousand feet in a single-engine Piper 6XT. A moment before, the engine had filled the cockpit with a solid rumbling, a vibration-filled sound that Carson Hill knew from hundreds of hours of flight time.

The engine-monitoring system panel hadn't given him a warning. The plane had shaken with what had felt like a small explosion. Then everything on the control board had just snapped down to zero. Black smoke had poured out of the engine compartment, covering the front windows with a thin, black film.

Now the smoke was gone and through the film he could see the tree-covered ridgeline directly ahead.

The slight creaking of metal, the faint sound of the wind rushing past the six-seater's windows. Nothing else broke the deadly quiet.

He forced down the panic threatening to overwhelm him.

"Goddammit! What the hell happened?" His voice seemed extra loud.

He took a deep breath. Losing control now would just make sure he died.

In his hands, the plane's controls felt heavy, unresponsive. His dead-stick training was from a book and a few sentences from his original flight instructor over three decades ago. He had never actually flown a plane without a working engine.

Around him, the dark blue September sky contrasted with the green forests and brown rocks of the Idaho wilderness below. Normally, he loved this easy flight. He'd done it every year at the same time for longer than he wanted to admit. Now everything below him looked like a nightmare in the making, ready to reach out and tear him apart.

The ridgeline loomed ahead, a wall of death. He wasn't clearing that ridge.

He forced himself to take a deep breath. Then, with shaking hands, he fought to get the plane into a very slow turn.

Nothing wanted to move.

The trees ahead filled everything in his sight.

He kept fighting the controls, forcing the plane to turn by almost sheer will. It took every bit of his strength, as if the plane had a mind of its own and actually wanted to crash into the trees and rocks.

Everything seemed to slow down.

Finally, the trees were no longer growing threats filling his vision, but instead were flashing past the wing's tip.

He bet he didn't miss the tops of the pines by more than a few feet.

Somehow, between deep, sobbing breaths of oil-tainted air, he got the plane leveled and back over the deep valley, headed downstream. Sweat ran down his face and into his eyes as he tried the restart sequence.

Nothing.

With almost no control, no engine, no place to land but into trees and rocks, he was as good as dead.

He pushed that thought away and grabbed the radio mike. "Mayday! Mayday!"

Silence.

No response from either the McCall or Cascade, Idaho airports.

He clicked on the global positioning emergency beacon. At least Search and Rescue would find him quickly.

Ahead, the narrow valley floor closed down tighter and tighter. He couldn't be more than a thousand feet above the stream and dropping faster than he wanted to think about. It was taking every bit of his strength to keep the plane flying and not stalling.

He wiped the sweat off his face with his sleeve and tried to get a good look at what lay ahead through the oil-smeared window. Sharp rocks and thick forests covered everything. At this speed, and without any real control, the plane would be torn apart on impact.

"Need an opening," he said. "Just give me an opening." His voice sounded loud and strained in the silence of the cockpit.

The valley narrowed ahead into a rock canyon, but over the edges of the rocks he could see a meadow beyond. If he could make the meadow, he might have a chance.

He tried to focus on the open area where the sun was shining, pushing the plane past the dark shadows of the rock canyon and into the light.

But he was dropping far too fast.

He tried feathering the controls to keep the plane up, but nothing seemed to work. Instead of something responsive in his hand, it felt like he was pushing against a stuck handle and pedals.

The rock walls now loomed ahead, a tiny opening leading to the sunshine beyond.

It was going to take a lot of luck to fit the plane through that narrow canyon opening. And after thirty-three years of playing professional poker, he didn't much believe in luck.

Then, quicker than he realized possible, he was in the canyon, the rocks flashing past. Ahead, the meadow seemed to call to him, the bright sunshine a beacon.

A tip of one wing caught the rock cliff face.

Before Carson had time to react or even cover his head and face, the small plane slammed into the rock wall.

***

STEVEN LEANED against a tall pine in the shade, trying to stay cool, watching impassively as Carson Hill's plane struggled to stay in the air.

From Steven's position on the top of the major ridgeline dividing the Cascade Valley from the central Idaho primitive area, he could see clear to the Middle Fork of the Salmon over thirty miles away. He had picked the spot just for that reason.

The day had turned beautiful, almost hot. He had waited patiently for six hours, slowly drinking bottles of water, until the signal had come in from the device he had planted in Carson's plane that told him Carson had started up his engine at the Scott airstrip deep inside the primitive area.

Steven felt no emotion as Carson Hill's six-seater Piper Cub barely escaped crashing into the hill below him. He simply watched as the plane drifted silently down the valley. Carson was full of all kinds of surprises. He shouldn't have been able to make that turn, not with his engine gone and his controls damaged in the small explosion Steven had set off in the plane's engine compartment.

The hillside below Steven had been the intended crash sight. More than likely the crash would still kill Carson, but it wasn't going to be close enough for Steven to retrieve Carson's key.

Steven shrugged. That was only a slight glitch in his plans. Too bad. He had wanted to take the key from Carson's dead, mangled body. There would have been a nice justice to that. But there would be other keys to give him that pleasure. There had been ten players in that poker game. Nine keys.

Steven dropped the small remote detonation device he had used to set off the explosion in Carson's plane into a three-foot-deep hole he had dug while waiting, then quickly filled the hole back up, covering it with pine needles. No point in carrying the device back down the mountain with him. No one would find it here, and even if they did, it couldn't be traced to him. He had left no detail to chance.

He trusted no one.

He had learned that lesson well.

Carson's key would survive the crash, and even with Carson dead, someone would have the key very shortly, then take Carson's position in the game.

If Steven had to kill that person, as well, so be it.

ABOUT THE AUTHOR

USA Today bestselling author Dean Wesley Smith published more than a hundred novels in thirty years and hundreds and hundreds of short stories across many genres.

He wrote a couple dozen *Star Trek* novels, the only two original *Men in Black* novels, Spider-Man and X-Men novels, plus novels set in gaming and television worlds. He wrote novels under dozens of pen names in the worlds of comic books and movies, including novelizations of a dozen films, from *The Final Fantasy* to *Steel* to *Rundown*.

He now writes his own original fiction under just the one name, Dean Wesley Smith. In addition to his upcoming novel releases, his monthly magazine called *Smith's Monthly* premiered October 1, 2013, filled entirely with his original novels and stories.

Dean also worked as an editor and publisher, first at Pulphouse Publishing, then for *VB Tech Journal*, then for Pocket Books. He now plays a role as an executive editor for the original anthology series *Fiction River*.

For more information about his work, go to www.deanwesleysmith. com, www.smithsmonthly.com or www.fictionriver.com.